BOOKS BY J.N. CHANEY

Renegade Star Series:

Renegade Star

Renegade Atlas

Renegade Moon

Renegade Lost

Renegade Fleet

Renegade Earth

Renegade Dawn

Renegade Children

Renegade Union

Renegade Empire (April 2019)

Renegade Prequels:

Nameless

The Constable

The Constable Returns (April 2019)

The Last Reaper Series:

The Last Reaper

Fear the Reaper (March 2019)

The Orion Colony Series:

Orion Colony

Orion Uncharted

Orion Awakened

Orion Protected (April 2019)

The Variant Saga:

The Amber Project

Transient Echoes

Hope Everlasting

The Vernal Memory

Standalone Books:

Their Solitary Way

The Other Side of Nowhere

STAY UP TO DATE

Chaney posts updates, official art, previews, and other awesome stuff on his website. You can also follow him on Instagram, Facebook, and Twitter.

Search for **JN Chaney's Renegade Readers** on Facebook to join the group where readers can come together and share their lives and interests, especially regarding Chaney's books.

For updates about new releases, as well as exclusive promotions, sign up for the VIP mailing list. Head there now to receive a free copy of *The Other Side of Nowhere.*

https://www.subscribepage.com/organic

Enjoying the series? Help others discover the *The Constable* series by leaving a review on Amazon.

THE CONSTABLE

BOOK 1 IN THE CONSTABLE SERIES

J.N. CHANEY

For Rob,
The smartest man I know

CONTENTS

1

TEST-TAKING PRODUCES A PECULIAR SILENCE. Every sound becomes deliberate and magnified. Even the tapping of a foot sends a signal.

I briefly wondered if it would be feasible to grade a test simply by watching the behavior of the test takers. There would always be anomalies, but I felt fairly certain I could deduce the performance of each student within a few percentage points. Clarence, for example, tapped his finger against the side of his seat when he was uncertain about an answer. I had observed this enough times to note it as a consistent behavior. However, not everyone showed such obvious tells or I simply didn't know them well enough to see it. In those cases, one could examine the movement of the eyes, the way their bodies shifted in their seats, or the rate of their breathing. I saw all of it, even without trying, and somehow I knew their thinking without fully understanding how I knew it.

As for my own test, I had finished it fifteen minutes prior but had yet to submit it. I sat at my desk, hands poised over the tablet as I waited to write down my final answer. I had completed it in my mind after only a few minutes, but turning in a test too quickly aroused suspicion of cheating, lucky guesses, or other interventions, and I had learned the hard way that wherever true excellence arose, suspicion was quick to follow.

I allowed my gaze to drift around the room, but only my gaze. If I had to turn my head, it meant I'd have to feign a stretch or another useless motion and, honestly, it was more effort than it was worth. I sat one row behind the middle to get a better view of the majority of the class, giving me the insight I craved into how my peers were faring with the assignment. Too far back and the teacher might think me a loafer. Too far forward and every action might draw unwanted attention.

Arthur was going to be done soon. He was in the front corner near the door. A poor position. Not only was his field of view limited, but it was the seat delinquents frequently sought when they arrived late to class and didn't want to appear disruptive. Arthur made enemies he didn't need by sitting there.

I noted the little jerk Arthur made when he entered his final review phase. He sat upright a bit harder, running his hand across the back of his neck.

I submitted my test and focused on Mr. Fenton. He was always a disinterested teacher. None of the eagle-eyed vigilance of Crenshaw or Mrs. Logan. Fenton's hands-off and eyes-down style had been helpful in avoiding confrontation for me so far, but today was different.

Fenton was more than just disinterested. He hunched on his desk over his table, his small frame nearly doubled in on itself as he did his best rendition of nonchalantly blocking any peering at his work.

I made a mental note to talk to him after class, if for no other reason than to express my observation about test sounds.

Arthur finished his review and sent his test. He gave himself a moment for a broad smile and a turn to revel in the satisfaction of "beating" everyone else.

I met his gaze as he turned, and he gave me a sly grin to show his dominance. "Arrogance is a poor face worn by a fool," my father told me once.

I was four years old at the time.

THE TEST NOW OVER, the students hurried to leave. As the final period of the day, Mr. Fenton's class always saw a quick exodus, and even Arthur remained behind only for the briefest of head-nodding and gloating. Within two minutes, all of the other students were out of the room.

I spent the time making a show of cleaning up my bag

and looking for something "important." I approached Mr. Fenton. "How are things?"

Fenton leaned over his tablet and looked up with a pinch at the corner of his right eye. "Oh, fine, fine. Thank you for asking. Always good to see the students taking a moment." He smiled.

I was unconvinced. Something was off, evidenced by the repetition of language and the positioning of the body. That pinch in the eye had to mean something.

"Good to hear, Mr. Fenton. See you tomorrow." I left the room and followed the wall absently with one hand as I considered the information I had just received.

I GREETED the secretary and provided my name.

She gave a curt nod. "What is this about?"

I took a seat to the side of the door. "A small issue with my last class. It won't take much of the headmaster's time."

Her expression remained that blank look of anyone forced into a service role without the underpinning passion. "I'll let him know."

No sooner had she finished speaking than the door opened. Headmaster Corrin gave a broad smile. His was genuine with a certain iron reinforcement, eyes engaged and brow raised slightly. Here was a man that cared about his job and its intrinsic purpose.

"Come inside, Alphonse."

I walked through the door and took a seat. Headmaster Corrin let the door close and sat on the edge of his desk. "What are we doing here today?"

"It's about Mr. Fenton. I'm certain he's stealing from the school."

Corrin drew himself up a little in shock. "Why would you even suggest that?"

I puzzled over the question for a moment. Proof was required, and my gut feeling wouldn't carry enough weight. "I overheard him," I said, knowing it was a lie. "He was on a call after class bragging about how he was 'getting away with it' and 'nobody suspected him in the slightest.'"

Corrin frowned his disapproval. "I don't think you knew what you were hearing."

His statement didn't entirely surprise me. I'd brought Corrin information about other illegal activities I'd noticed in the past, largely among the students. These observations ranged from drug use to sexual harassment. Some things I didn't report on, such as cheating or skipping class, but the larger and more dangerous activities always found their way to his ear. I'd done this for several months, slowly building our trust, though I couldn't say why I was doing it.

"I'm not expecting you to take my word," I continued. "Open an investigation on Fenton and find your proof. Quietly, if you must, to save your reputation."

Corrin sighed then breathed quietly for a moment before speaking. "There have been a few misappropriations of funds, I'll give you that. These were small at first, and it seems like a system error is unlikely." He seemed to be thinking out loud.

I waited for the *but*.

"But accusing a teacher is a serious matter. The accusation alone could destroy the man's career. I won't hear of it. Anything else?"

"I think some of the students may have been cheating. If you review Mr. Fenton's pad, there may be evidence."

"Of cheating, or something else?" he asked, cocking his brow.

"Yes," I said, simply.

Corrin walked back to the door. "I'll look into the matter. I trust you won't be speaking to anyone else?"

I stood up. "Thank you for your attention on this matter, Headmaster."

It was out of my hands and, at this point, I felt satisfied.

2

FOUR DAYS LATER, I was called into the headmaster's office during lunch period. The secretary—a stuffy woman by the name of Ms. Clare Dofaine—indicated I was free to eat while I waited for Headmaster Corrin to arrive.

I took the opportunity to actually enjoy my meal for once. In the cafeteria, it was important to move along swiftly. The tables only supported so many students at any given time, leaving many waiting in line to be seated. This provided a sense of urgency, likely an intentional choice by the school board to cycle as many students through as possible in under an hour. It kept us from returning for second servings, as it happened, and consequently lowered the school's costs. I always endeavored to be done within ten minutes, before the next group could arrive. This gave me better vantages to observe and avoid being boxed in by the press of bodies.

Regardless, the quiet of the headmaster's office provided an interesting change of pace.

I slowly ate the balanced but not always appetizing offerings of protein and carbs in the meal and let myself take in features of the office that were normally at the periphery when Headmaster Corrin was there.

The right wall was bare, save for a window with a blind. This looked out into the grounds and allowed the headmaster to view some of the sports and intramurals that took place below.

The left wall held a bookcase with a few precious real paper books. The titles related to pedagogy of a time long past. Baudelaire, Rosseau, Teffling, and the still-living Herickson.

The back wall contained several plaques and awards. These weren't too impressive, the kind of mid-tier acknowledgements given to a fair but unremarkable public servant. Lists of educational achievements that amounted to little more than completing courses and attending talks.

A portrait of an admiral from the past was the only true stand-out in the décor. He wore a placid expression meant to show strength, wisdom, or resolve. The right epaulette featured fringe, a star, and a bar.

I sat quietly, looking at the image for some time. Despite my intent to slow down, the meal was still completed by the time Headmaster Corrin arrived.

He slipped in through the smallest opening he could make in the doorway. No sooner was his frame through the entrance than he had closed it behind him. He seated himself at the desk and sighed.

"You were right, Alphonse. I called up a log on Fenton's personal pad from the last several weeks. Our official reasoning involved an investigation into cheating, as you suggested, by some students with unusually high testing scores."

"I see," I replied with a soft nod.

He called up a display and projected it where I could see. "There was nothing unusual in the access or activity logs on the pad. The resource usage was another thing." He pulled down the first projection and it was replaced with another readout with highlighted peaks along a graph. "Here is the problem. These peaks of processing power correspond with times when the recreational fund was accessed and transfers were made."

He gave me a worried look and closed out the projection. "The academy appreciates you bringing this to our attention. Mr. Fenton was relieved of his position a few minutes ago."

A sudden knock on the door had Corrin jumping to his feet. The door opened and a woman I recognized from a photo on the headmaster's desk came in. "Rupert, you forgot your lunch this morning." She held a sealed container in her left hand and tugged on her coat with her right even as she pressed the door shut behind her.

She paused as she saw me, and her smile dropped for a moment before it grew wider. "I see. I didn't realize you had a student." She nodded to me. "My apologies." Then she turned back to Corrin and said, "Here you go," before setting the container on his desk.

There was a difference in her posture as she turned to the door. A rigidness to her step and a tremble in her hand now free of the container. "I'll let you get back to work." She nodded at me. "Be good now."

The door closed, a hint of vanilla and the slight sound of fabric shifting remaining behind. Corrin sat down again, taking a moment before continuing our conversation. "If you see anything else, let me know," he said, looking at me. "Though I hope there will be no further incidents like this. You are excused."

I stood and took a step toward the door. "Are you sure you want to know about anything I notice?" I asked him.

The headmaster was distracted as he opened his lunch. His eyes lit up and he paused unexpectedly as he peered at the contents. "What? Oh, yes. Anything you come across that strikes you as unusual. You've done a fine job of reporting. We've expelled fourteen students and now a teacher because of you, and the school is better off." He paused. "So, yes, keep it coming."

I nodded beside the door, then turned to face him completely, placing both hands behind my back. "Your wife is cheating on you."

For a moment, Corrin did nothing. Then his eyes narrowed, and he spoke in a choked whisper. "What?"

I let the words linger in the air, knowing it would take him time to process. "She's having an affair. She's headed to meet with her lover now. If you follow her, you will see."

Corrin said nothing at first. His eyes flickered between me and the door, a growing fear in them as he began to understand what I'd told him. "G-Get out. Get out of this office at once."

I did as he asked, not bothering with a response. I knew I was right, and it wouldn't take long before the headmaster saw the truth as well.

———

I RETURNED to class the following morning, ready for another mundane day of so-called learning. I was barely in the door when Ms. Dofaine stopped me from the hall and motioned for me to approach. "The headmaster wants to speak to you." She pointed in the direction of his office. "This way, please."

I followed and watched the sideways glances from the students headed into their respective classes.

I suspected I knew what this was about, given our previous exchange.

The halls were quiet for a while before I arrived at the headmaster's office. His door was cracked, as though it were waiting for me to find it.

Corrin stood inside, and I could already see the unsteady posture, a nervousness in his stance. He had the look of a man distraught and overcome with too many thoughts, his gaze reminiscent of the admiral on his shelf. I closed the door and noticed an empty garment bag strapped across the inside handle.

The headmaster's shirt was rumpled, his tie missing, and the faint smell of booze and cheap food rose from the nearby trash.

I took a seat and waited a moment. The headmaster remained fixed at the window. His breaths were uneven, and several times he straightened briefly before slumping and resigning himself to leaning against the wall.

A band of light skin revealed the absence of his ring. "You saw them," I said.

He looked away from the window then, his eyes sunken and red at the edges. He struggled for a step and slumped into his chair, pausing for several seconds before finally giving me a single defeated nod. "I followed her," he admitted. "After the last time you and I met. I called up the car service and tracked her." He sat back in the chair and stared at the ceiling, sniffling. "One search led to another. She went to a neighborhood far from home. Some apartment building. When she finally returned to our house, I confronted her, showed her the records . . . demanded an answer."

"Did she admit to it?" I asked.

"Not at first, but it didn't take much to get her to talk," he recalled. "It was like she"—he paused, almost searching for the right words—"like she wanted to tell me and all it took was a nudge. She confessed right there in the foyer. Two years, she said to me. For two years, she'd been seeing a former teacher of *this* institution. A colleague and man I thought of as a friend."

I nodded, a sense of pride welling in me. I'd always liked the headmaster. He was a fair man, professional and courteous. Unlike some educators, he took his job seriously but didn't allow himself the preening self-assuredness that led to conceit.

"I'm glad I was able to help." I stood up and approached the door. "I will do my best to keep you informed of anything else I come across."

Corrin croaked out a syllable. "No." His gaze gained a remarkable concentration but did not move away from the desk. It looked as if he was trying to see through both it and the floor beneath. "No, Alphonse. I don't want you telling me anything. You're—"

I sat back down and waited for his thought to conclude.

"—being transferred," he finally said. "You will be going to our sister school, Quintell Academy. I'm sorry, but you leave tomorrow morning. First thing, before classes start. Return to your room right now and pack your things."

That was when I saw it—that the gaze he had been giving wasn't filled with sadness at the betrayal of his wife, but of something else entirely. Since I had entered, I'd felt him acting at a different cadence, a distant tone in his voice that I'd mistaken for distraction. In truth, it had been his way of separating us, emotionally distancing himself from what he thought he had to do.

I'd been so foolish to think that sharing his wife's affair

with him would prove beneficial. How could I have been so arrogant? Of course, it could only lead here.

My father's words echoed in my mind, and all at once I understood. *Arrogance is a poor face worn by a fool.*

The quaking in Corrin's voice and the slight tremble in his hands were not anger at the misdeeds of his wife or the betrayal of his former colleague. It was fear. The same fear I'd seen in my father when he sent me away. The same fear that I'd tried so hard to avoid.

A brief moment of that day flashed in my mind. Father, angry with me for telling him about his brother's behaviors, not wanting to believe it but knowing it was the truth. Mother clinging behind him and crying.

I had intruded on the headmaster's life. Without knowing it or understanding it, I had invaded his privacy and turned his world inside out. It was happening again, and now I would have to leave. I was a victim of my own pride, impaled upon my ego.

"Leave, Mr. Malloy. Just . . . leave." He thrust a hand at the door and leaned heavily with the other planted on the desk. His eyes had not moved.

"Thank you for the time here, Headmaster," I stated, turning away and walking out the door.

I saw the secretary feigning interest in her screen. A security officer tried to look both official and invisible against the far wall. Everyone would soon know that Alphonse Malloy was being sent away. Word would spread through the halls as gossip always does, and theories would emerge in a matter of days.

I walked to the hall, keeping a normal pace, and soon returned to the dorms. I tried my best to ignore the outside world, to focus on what would come next. Somehow, I sensed two men in the distance, far behind me, always keeping my pace. Security officials, perhaps, tasked with keeping an eye on the troubled boy with too much to say. I could tell they were there, but I didn't know how.

3

THE NEXT MORNING, I found myself in front of the headmaster's door. Classes were still an hour away. It was clear that my removal was to occur before the normal day resumed.

The hallways were still dark. The only light came from inside the office and a few emergency track lights.

I could hear voices. One was obviously Corrin's, but the other I didn't recognize. I couldn't make out any specific words, but the tones were adversarial.

The secretary wasn't even there. The only other presence was of the security official that had brought me from the dorms. He stood near the entrance and waited to escort me to wherever my next destination would be.

The argument inside the office was short. Only a few words were exchanged before the door was thrust open. Corrin stood in the doorway with far more purpose than he'd expressed the day before. Gone was the slump and the tremors in the hands.

He gave me a fixed gaze and a quick nod. As he gestured inside the office, I noted that he seemed more upset at his visitor than me. Or perhaps it was an anger he had come to after the despair of his wife's affair had subsided.

The second man did not strike me as a school official. He stood too rigid and his shoes were too ostentatious—a thin silver trim against the tip, tapping the floor with each step. They didn't seem comfortable or well-worn, but rather as though he'd barely worn them at all.

Corrin introduced me. "Mr. Malloy, we are joined by a representative from our sister school, Quintell Academy. This is Mr. Black."

I gave the strange, tall man a quick nod and sat down as indicated. Corrin stood to the side of his desk and Mr. Black took up the headmaster's usual position behind it. The role reversal certainly could explain Corrin's anger.

Corrin did his best to look like he was in charge and in control, his posturing coming off as little more than nervous theatrics to Quintell's unmoving figure.

Mr. Black smiled at me. "Hello. I'm here to interview you briefly before we leave. Consider it a useful tool for placing you in the right classes and programs at Quintell Academy."

Corrin balked at the thought. "I've never heard of such a placement interview. The transfer is simple and already—"

"Mr. Corrin," Mr. Black interrupted, "this exchange would be easier if you would excuse yourself for the interview process. Thank you for the kind use of your office." All of this was without a sideways glance at the headmaster. Mr. Black also outmaneuvered any complaint or resistance from Corrin before it could even be raised.

Corrin frowned slightly, but it was enough to show his discomfort with the old man. He proceeded to take his leave, but paused at the door. He took another look at Mr. Black, furrowing his unmistakably thick brow. "I hope you'll be quick about this, sir," said the headmaster.

Mr. Black said nothing and gave no indication that he cared. His emotionless face revealed nothing to me, not even in the slightest, and I found this most troubling.

Black's eyes drifted to mine as Corrin shut the door behind me. The old man did not pierce or glare at me but simply observed. He had the face and demeanor of someone you could meet a dozen times and still know nothing about him, with no discernable features to tell his story. No scars or blemishes, and only enough wrinkles to suggest that he was over forty. He kept a dispassionate energy about him, as though he could be doing anything else at this moment.

He moved slightly to bring up a display on the console. The letterhead for Quintell Academy shone bright against the standard lights of the office.

Mr. Black smiled, a short bit of courtesy. "Mr. Malloy, good to meet you. How is the day treating you?" he asked. "I'm sure you're anxious to get this transfer over with."

I noted the shift in tone and the way he transitioned from statement to polite questions. "You're not from Quintell." I matched his previous tone, leaving no room for maneuvering in my statement to him.

That affected smile presented itself again. "I am here to talk with you. That is all you need to be concerned with."

"The only reason this is happening is because the headmaster prefers I disappear," I stated.

"I suppose he does," said Mr. Black.

The answer surprised me. I had expected resistance to my accusation, given the seriousness of its implication. "If you know that, then why are you going along with it?" I asked.

"I have no reason to interfere with Headmaster Corrin's work," said Mr. Black. "Nor should you, in point of fact."

"How do you mean?" I asked.

"I don't know the details of your behavior, nor do I care enough to learn. However, what I see leaves me with enough information to deduce that you would be better off elsewhere, Mr. Malloy. In this case, as a member of Quintell Academy."

I settled in, allowing myself to observe the whole room and take in the information without focusing on anything specific. Again, mirroring the energy and affectations of Mr. Black. "I know you're not from Quintell, or any other academy. What are you actually doing here?"

"That man was happy to hear your theories in the past, I suspect," continued Mr. Black, paying no mind to my accusations or questions. "He likely enjoyed having you around to feed him information on the goings-on inside this institution. But the way he looks at you, the way he acts around you"—he paused, presenting a smile—"you've made him afraid of you."

I said nothing.

"Shall we begin?" asked Mr. Black. "Question one. What is your name?"

I noted that my name was already printed on the screen, along with several file names that my records and transcripts must have included. Also, Corrin had introduced me when I came in. "Alphonse Malloy."

Mr. Black continued. "Question two. Have you ever committed an act of violence that was not to defend yourself or another?"

Despite the leading wording, it was still clear that the question was meaningless; the answer was known in advance and also irrelevant. "I've never so much as raised a hand against anyone." I waited a beat before continuing, long enough to disrupt the back and forth but before it was an interruption. "How do you know if I'm telling you the truth?"

Mr. Black gave no reaction to the delay or the follow-up question. He simply continued. "Question three. How old are you?"

"Fourteen years, three months, five days."

"Question four. What is your earliest memory?"

There was something in that last question. A tiny hint of a spark in Mr. Black's eyes. The transition was slight, but there was no way he would know the answer this time.

I took a second, momentarily letting my own gaze shift as memories returned. "I was in a car, my mother and father in the front. It was sunny. Late afternoon and spring. I was two years old."

"Question five." He punched a button on the display and an image replaced the academy letterhead. It remained visible for two seconds then went back to the letterhead. "List everything you just saw." His tone was a touch eager but more clinical than the previous one.

"The foreground is a busy street. Forty-seven people total. They are of varying heights and proportions. There are three couples: two hugging and one engaged in a kiss. There are Sixteen unique hairstyles and twelve colors." I took a quick breath. "Six figures are fighting or at least at odds. There are twelve buildings. The architecture suggests early century Berrinian. There are five animals: a dog, two rodents, and two cats. The yellow cat is giving chase to a rodent."

Mr. Black listened to the descriptions without comment or reaction. He took no notes. "Question six. What would you like to do with the rest of your life?" The question was once again asked as a formality with no regard for the answer.

The question caught me by surprise, and for a brief moment I shifted in my chair. "I would . . ." I paused, unable to find the words. "I am going . . ." Again, nothing. It wasn't a question of fact but opinion, and I had no answer ready to give.

Mr. Black dropped his smile and frowned. "You've never considered the future?" The phrasing suggested something, but I couldn't place what.

"My parents were programmers. Maybe that." The

answer seemed flat and hollow, even to me, and I knew it was a lie.

Mr. Black turned off the letterhead projection. "Does programming interest you?"

I heard myself mutter, "I don't know."

Mr. Black nodded and stood up. "Very well, then. That's all. I've everything I need from the test. You will depart for Quintell Academy at once." He walked to the door and paused. "Good luck, Mr. Malloy."

He looked at me in that moment. Actually, truly, at me. Not around or through, but into my eyes. It was more than any of the teachers had done, more than the other students, and I didn't know what to make of it.

4

I CONSIDERED the gravity of my situation as I strapped into the seat of the shuttle. Around me, new travelers and weary frequenters busied themselves with pre-flight rituals. I went through the motions of my own checklist while considering the past day and beyond.

I realized I was in a memory freefall when the launch warning beeped. A voice spoke through the individual speakers in the seat and listed the final checklist items. "Launch in five minutes, expect ignition turbulence. All crew strap in. All passengers are green lit."

I was disturbed to realize I had memory-dumped myself through the verticalization stage. My legs were above my chest, my back parallel with the ground. It was a strange feeling, gravity weighing you down in this position, but it was one I'd experienced a few times before. It was far easier to load the shuttle horizontally and then move it into position on the staged boosters. This both ensured comfort for the passengers in boarding and compliance for takeoff, as anyone that failed to strap properly would tumble as the zenith moved past a grade of fifty degrees.

"Three-minute call. Second stage ignition ready."

There was a deep rumbling from below and around as the primary booster built pressure and the secondary systems were super-cooled to avoid depressurizing before they were needed. I lacked the engineering prowess to understand exactly what was needed to establish a space elevator on the planet, but part of me wished the government had chosen to build one.

"Fuel pressure maximized. Beginning initial acceleration."

It was hard to look around at this stage of a launch. The g-forces began to build and push me back in the seat. My field of vision was also drastically reduced by the full helmet. Minors, which I was counted as, were required for insurance reasons to be fully suited for takeoffs. It was an outdated and, frankly, ridiculous policy. I was allowed to remove the gear once we achieved orbit, the one place where it would do any good.

Still, the helmet did give some extra support on the neck. It didn't take too many launches to start seeing demyelination of the spinal cord. That and the low gravity demineralization were reasons to avoid constant travel on commercial transports.

"Activating stage two propulsion and accelerating to escape velocity."

My idle fascination with the specifics of extra orbital flight were not enough to keep me from being annoyed that I was also forced to listen to the play-by-play. It was assumed that, psychologically, minors were less prone to panic if they knew exactly where the ship was in the launch process.

Fear of exploding in atmosphere or crashing via bad telemetry was almost laughable. The last mishap of that sort was a half-century past and attributed to impact with a falling object. A fluke so rare they didn't even institute additional scanning protocols to counter it.

"Final stage firing, leaving orbit en route to dock with designated transport vessel."

Another beep and the controls for the screen in front of me unlocked. I saw Provinka City drift away in the onboard replay. Direct broadcasting of the on-site cameras was blocked during launch. They were prone to sudden cut-outs at velocity shifts, which could cause panic to a young viewer live. So the footage was recorded and edited to give an impression of a smooth takeoff. The final blanket for the poor psyche of space travelers from long ago. Regulations and safety measures didn't evolve with sensibilities.

The imagery of Provinka City reminded me of my sole experience with space flight. I was ten and recently removed from home by my father. It was "recommended" that I would be better off in boarding school off-planet. I had been sent systems away, literally lightyears away so they could feel safe.

Even then, years ago and one of my first experiences outside of my parents' watchful care, the safety features for minors had been annoying. The video playback was more interesting to me, though. I recalled the way my home had drifted below me, growing smaller and becoming obscured by clouds, then seeing the curve of the atmosphere and finally the darkness of space. I knew, subjectively, in what direction my original system lay, but I hadn't bothered to identify the specific star. It was just a place that I had been.

My guardian *ad litem* at the time served from the moment I was brought aboard the shuttle and discharged when I left the port in Provinka City and became a ward of the academy. I was old enough this time that no such guardian was appointed, or perhaps Mr. Black was named such. He was not on the shuttle, which I didn't find surprising. Whatever organization was behind him clearly had other transport options.

"Free cabin movement is permitted until docking with the Heavy Hand in approximately one hour."

I removed the helmet so I could look around. I was distracted from my thoughts of Mr. Black and his clearly made-up cover as a representative of Quintell Academy. The hum of conversation from the other passengers took precedent.

An old man shambled to the front of the craft and was first in line to start requesting favors of the crew. An implant blinked on his left shoulder, visible through the loose shirt he was wearing. The implants were meant to compensate for strain from frequent travel and as recorders for medical data.

Long-term understanding of the effects of space flight required a constant influx of data.

I considered the ramifications of the device for a moment, as well as the research that went into it. I recalled reading some notes from my mother's terminal months before my expulsion from her life. She was developing some kind of selection algorithm for test subjects. I recalled the notation, but nothing of the code. I found it difficult to maintain information with no relevant reference point.

That brought me back to Mr. Black and this morning. The series of questions was a puzzle in itself. The memory assessment of the image made sense in one fashion but left me wondering what else could have been behind it. Why had a man like that come to see a student like me? His observation skills had been intriguing, the way he gleaned specifics about my relationship with the headmaster and our history. It was impressive, and I wanted to speak with him again, though part of me suspected I would never have the chance.

What had me baffled was the final question. The question had its own set of possible implications. An emphasis on curriculum was obvious. Perhaps it was posed to ascertain if continuing education was worthwhile for a discipline case. It was my inability to answer the question that was a problem.

I had thought about it before. At least, I supposed I had. By my age, I had been encouraged to write a dozen essays on the topic. To make art or give speeches about a future career or place I would prefer to live.

I hadn't answered the question dishonestly in the past, I

just hadn't put any real truth in it. Where I would go was where I would end up. What I would do was whatever I would do. These responses changed based on the person asking because I doubted they cared about the answer. It was an assignment. Work to keep the school day moving.

Many people find a talent they possess and expand. Others stumble into an opportunity and stay because they don't apply decision-making. Still others follow in the path of their parents or well-off relatives, repeating patterns they have seen work.

The answer I gave to Mr. Black followed that pattern. It sounded like the kind of answer he wanted, but it clearly wasn't. I knew as I spoke that it was wrong. What I didn't really understand was why.

What did I want out of life? What was the future? By many accounts, I had at least ten years of schooling or more to go through. But knowing the answer to this question shaped many of those years. If I acknowledged that the question had weight to it, why didn't I have an answer?

Worse, why didn't I care enough to have one?

A crew member approached me. "Can we get you anything?" His voice was remarkably free of the condescension I heard while boarding and being strapped in.

"How long until we dock?" I decided to probe for more personal information from the man behind the Paul nametag.

"It will be fifty more minutes and then twenty of seated time while the docking takes place. Do you mean until we hit the slip tunnel or the whole journey?" He was leaning against the seat now, giving me his full attention.

I calculated the trip would be roughly another two hours of undocking, taxiing, and eventual landing. All told, it would be evening before I was on Meridian in the Androsia system. "Any dense fruits you have, and a water, would be fine. Thank you."

He slapped the headrest on the seat. "You're a smart traveler. Lot of these people will be squirming during the other strap-down phases. Nervous drinkers always have nervous bladders. You sure you don't want something a little extra?" He gave a broad, exaggerated wink.

It was unlikely he was baiting me into requesting alcohol. I took the gesture as best I could, mirroring his friendly energy. "Maybe next time. I'm still tipsy from breakfast."

He laughed. "I'll be right back with your snack and water."

Meanwhile, the frequenter from before had taken his seat three rows back from mine. It was difficult to observe while sitting as they had placed me near the front of the shuttle. I waited for Paul to return so I would have an excuse to look around without appearing obvious. People were always quick to adjust behavior when they thought they were being watched.

Paul returned with a water and two packets of a freeze-dried fruit medley. He handed me one of the waters and a packet, then opened the other himself. "Mind if I chat with you while we wait?"

I smiled and opened my own packet. "Thanks. I've not done a lot of traveling. Got any interesting things to share?" I stood up and leaned against the seat, forcing him to position in front of me so I could see the frequenter over his right shoulder.

He started explaining some mishaps and interesting details about journeys he had taken. I let the sound fade to the periphery. From the moment I saw the frequenter quick to get drink orders in, I had become curious about him.

It is one thing to have a preflight drink or to like to mingle. To do both expressed a level of nerves that needed explanation. I could have written it off as jitters if he wasn't a frequenter. It was possible he had experienced recent trauma or a personal loss that had him off.

The lack of any secondary characteristics made that unlikely. He had done everything he could to avoid making specific eye contact now that he was back at his seat.

He looked around quickly.

I made a point to react to the tale Paul was relating but not draw too much attention. The frequenter looked my way and then swept past. He had finished one drink and went right into the next. The crew serving him didn't hesitate to supply him two-deep just to stop being called over.

I noticed he was sweating and kept checking the time. He dropped a drink with a clatter.

Paul was quick to react. "Sorry. Sir? I'll get that for you."

The man was slapping liquid off his sleeve and swearing. Paul tried to pick up the container and wipe up the excess liquid as it pooled. For a brief moment, the implant under the man's shirt went dark and he jiggled it until it lit up.

The frequenter's implants were powered through bio converters. Either the man had died briefly, or it was fake. It all became clear then; he was a stowaway, probably on false credentials.

Paul finished cleaning up the mess and returned to me. "Looks like we're about to dock. You can check it out on your screen."

I flicked on the screen and strapped myself back in. The Heavy Hand, a powerful cylinder with large mounting brackets, came into view. Patches of the ship held enormous cargo containers and there was even a smaller asteroid secured in one spot. The shuttle docked and mounted to a smaller ring of clamps near the center.

Most of the docking procedure was invisible to the monitor, but I took a moment to flip through the feeds and see more of the attached cargo. The Union supply network was impressive. My father would complain that its bureaucracy was slow, and many rules were outdated and staid. "But they keep the transports synchronized," he would often conclude.

Docking completed and there was a sudden shift in the gravity. Being attached to the far larger mass of the Heavy Hand stabilized the gravity inside the cabin and everything felt heavier and more real.

I watched intently as a green light pierced the darkness at the nose of the transport. It grew in intensity until it was hard to make out any details of the transport amidst the brilliant emerald glow.

I switched cameras to the rear and saw the ship gradually enveloped in the glow as the tear continued to form. There was a great buildup of momentum from inside the transport cylinder.

All around, a magnificent light shone as we entered the phenomenon known as slipspace.

I had to admit, it was quite beautiful.

5

It was mid-evening when I finally arrived at the campus of Quintell Academy. The time duration on Meridian swung close to a thirty-hour day. There would be some hours of light left. Fortunately, it was still spring in the hemisphere of the new school.

Moving from one continent to the other had nothing on interplanetary travel. The stars were different, each sun a different size, and the temperatures were on a different range. The body tried to adjust and get into the necessary circadian cycle. Sometimes, the transition was easy. Other times, it took weeks to adjust.

A woman waited for me as I left the bus and my luggage was retrieved. She was stout and in her late forties, with a short-cropped haircut that gave hints of a military back-ground. Her shoes were scuffed and less than formal. The incongruity with her presentation almost made me laugh. It would be unthinkable to see a student in such disarray at my former school, let alone a staff member, but if this academy had any merit to its name, I likely wouldn't be here.

She greeted me with an awkward wave that was part handshake and part salute. "Welcome to Quintell Academy, Mr. Malloy. I'm Dr. Maevik, a psychometrician. I'll be taking you to your room."

"Psychometrician? So, you're in charge of assessments?" I asked.

"That's right," she said.

I gathered my two bags and stood ready to be directed. "Well, then, lead the way, Doctor."

Maevik swept into position in front of me and started talking loudly to direct her voice behind, even though it was quiet and I had no problem hearing her. "You can call me Cams. We're pretty informal around here. No Doctor necessary."

I said nothing, but she seemed to take the silence as a form of agreement. The walk to the room wasn't very long. The dormitories were on the edge of the campus to minimize noise and separate the school environment from the living area.

She snapped her heels and turned at the door to the dormitory. "You'll be given a room key and assignment by the floor manager. His room is the first you will see on the right. Your floor manager will also be in charge of directing any facilities problems you have."

I shouldered my bookbag and opened the door. "Do I report to an office or a person for classes tomorrow?"

She rocked back on her heel and then laughed. "Oh, right. There is an office in the main building that you will hit first thing. They'll sort that for you."

"Thank you," I said and entered. The hallway was sparse and an off-white that left me to wonder if the paint had faded from age or darkened from neglect. I turned the corner to the right and knocked. A minute later, the door opened with a sharp jolt.

An older boy stood there. His hair was shaggy and his lean frame filled out his clothes poorly, leaving everything about him looking rushed and transitional. "Yeah? What?" he managed.

"Alphonse Malloy, new student. I need a room assignment." I kept it direct and ignored his lack of tact.

"Oh, that." He shut the door and I waited for a few minutes before it opened again. In the interim, he had retrieved some clothes and a key. "Follow me, we've got you over in 109 at the end of the hall. You gotta come back out this way, though, to leave. The doors at the ends get jammed."

He walked the distance with me, going past a series of doors with odd spots and discolorations along the frames. We stopped at the end and he tried to hand me the key.

I set down a bag and took the key from him.

"Well?" He gestured at the door and then slumped against the wall.

I slid the key card through the slot and watched as the

system slowly confirmed the entry. It took almost twelve seconds to cycle green. I shoved the latch and entered. Behind me, the floor manager produced a tablet that he must have had stashed in a large pocket. "Bed, desk, lamp, dresser, all in great condition. One key issued. Sign it."

He thrust the pad at me with a waiver for the room hastily filled out. I glanced at the furnishings, threadbare and worn but all well enough, then signed the document.

He glanced at the signature, shut off the pad, and began to walk away. He turned back after a few steps. "Hey, if you need anything, don't bother. I'm not going to try and they're not gonna get it anyway. Just leave me alone. We clear?"

I nodded. He strode down the hall and back to his own room. I entered mine and set down my bags. Overall, the room was only slightly smaller than my previous one. The quality of the furnishings was a larger issue. Everything was worn and chipped. It didn't look as if anything had been replaced or touched up in a decade. Maybe since before I was born.

I unpacked my bookbag and sorted the contents into the desk, then I hung up my garments and placed the remainder in the dresser. My clothing consisted of five uniforms, two pairs of shoes, and some sundries. The desk held my three personal books and my pad.

I turned on the pad and set it to local time and declination, then synced it with my watch. With everything put away, I had nothing to do until the following day and my new class assignments. My pad was on the dormitory's network, but I had no access to the academy intranet. It took a few minutes of looking, but I found the campus curfew listed in a promotional page. I had several hours before the night lockdown. Assuming the floor manager cared for such a thing.

With nothing to study or anything specific to do, I decided to familiarize myself with the academy grounds. The hallway was clear of any other students, and despite the unkempt nature of the facility, the dorm rooms appeared soundproof.

The campus wasn't too different from my previous one. There was a dormitory split into several floors and an auxiliary building. Previously, the floors had been arranged by seniority ranking with the auxiliary for special students—children of dignitaries, large donors, and the like. It was hard to say how the arrangement here would work, but I suspected it wasn't likely to be graced by the sons of dignitaries. This was a school for transfer students, I suspected, each of us deemed unworthy by our former academies. Strange, since we had already been sent away by families that didn't want us.

After the dorms, there was a central administration building, which also housed core curriculum rooms and teacher offices. Two other classroom buildings stood flanking the center building. They seemed to be, from exterior indications, STEM, humanities, and history buildings. There was also a track and a gymnasium split into multiple sections for different games and activities.

I wandered into the gymnasium and watched other students practicing different sports. The facilities all showed a lack of attention I found concerning. Nothing was broken, outright, but many things were in advanced states of disrepair. There was a pervasive laissez-faire sense here, with the expectant result.

From observing the other students, I noticed that only a few had anything close to a uniform. Even then, it was one or two pieces with the others a mismatch of plain clothes and severely altered uniform fragments. I sat in the bleachers of one of the athletics rooms, observing, when I was approached by two students.

The taller one wore the remains of a uniform blazer over a t-shirt and sagging pants. He had one sleeve rolled beyond the elbow and the other was frayed from some kind of compulsive behavior. "Hey," he shouted up at me. "Looking good there, newbie. Nobody told you we keep it real 'round here?"

The shorter one with the muscular legs and thick neck chuckled. He wore an a-shirt over his t-shirt in a clashing set of orange with green that was an affront to the senses. His shorts were once a longer pair of pants that had been cut and folded and pinned in the front and were loose in the back. "You think he knows anything about how it goes down in Quintell, Manson? He looks like he's never been away from home a minute of his life."

They split up at the bottom of the bleachers and approached row by row, drifting further apart to flank me. The one identified as Manson took a seat uncomfortably close to me and leaned into my face. The shorter one hedged me in with one leg and hovered forward.

Manson spoke in the same shout he had used at the base of the bleachers but within a few inches of my face. "Transfer student, Gil. Mid-semester. You know what that means?"

Gil swayed at the hips, making tiny gyrations at my right ear and dipping down toward my head with each thrust. "Sounds like something real bad went down. Think he slugged a student or snogged a teacher?"

Simpletons, the both of them, easily riled by insults. Better to stay calm.

Manson pushed in even closer, switching to what I assumed was his best menacing whisper. "I think you got that the other way around. Looks to me like the type that acts out at authority."

He carried himself on his left leg, placing too much of his weight with no sense as to the balance. If I wanted, I could capitalize on that.

Gil slapped his extended knee with his forward hand, leaving the one behind me unseen. Each slap got a little louder as he staccato-style fired off his next taunt. "Gotta be something stupid. Strike policies and all."

Manson wiped his nose with the fraying sleeve and then flicked it across my face and chest.

I still pretended the two didn't exist as I sat there quietly.

Gil broke out in hysterics and slapped me on the back a few times. "Oh, Manson. I don't know that'll come out in a wash." He punctuated his statement by pinching his right nostril and blowing a wad of gunk onto my pants.

It was Manson's turn to laugh and slap me, each time a little harder. "Probably best if you get out of these dirty rags as quick as possible, eh?"

I kept a calm appearance, acting as though I hadn't noticed the freshly thrown snot on my clothes. "I'm glad you're so concerned about my well-being," I remarked, feigning a smile. "It's nice to be treated so well on my first day, but try not to worry too much about me. The staff seems to be monitoring the gym, though, which means we're all safe and sound. Isn't that nice of them?"

"Monitoring?" echoed Gil. He looked around, but saw no sign of any teachers. "What are you talking about?"

I nodded to the wall with the exit door, near one of the offices. "Just over there, do you see it? There's a small camera," I said, as though it should be obvious. "It must be new if you're unaware of it." I let out a sigh and smiled warmly. "It's so nice that the staff cares enough to keep us safe, don't you think?"

Manson swung back to me, an embarrassed look on his face. "Crap," he muttered. "When did they install that?"

Before Gil could answer, another voice rang out, speeding up the bleachers. "You two idiots looking to fail out again?"

They both snapped their heads in the direction of the approaching student. It was a fair-haired boy that seemed a bit older than either of them. He had a lanky build but held his posture with an elasticity. He seemed almost to be made out of rubber the way he swayed and bobbed as he came up the rows, sporting a cocky grin while wearing a simple shirt and pants outfit with bright-colored athletic shoes. He was self-possessed and alert in comparison to the other two and their wincing gazes.

Manson sat me up with his back hand and scooted away a bit. "Just introducing ourselves to the new guy, Vance."

Gil bounced to the side, keeping more than a row distance between himself and Vance. "We were updating him about the dress code here."

Vance nodded. "I see that. You want me to get you the answers for Balner's chem test the end of the week? You can't be doing a disciplinary before. They'll force you to solo proctor it."

The two self-styled thugs moved further away and started to retreat down the bleacher rows. Manson turned back and fixed me with an intense but unconvincing glare. "We'll see you later." He turned his attention to Vance. "We want those answers. Tomorrow. This one can have a bit before we get back around."

Vance gave a dismissive wave. "Yeah, yeah. We get it. Just see I don't hear anything out of you two before next week or you might find yourselves relying on your own brains to pass a class. Dark thought, my friends."

He offered a cloth and sat down a few seats to the side of me. "I'm Vance, if you didn't catch that. They were Manson and Gil. They aren't all bad, just examples of what happens when you buy into the idea that there needs to be a hierarchy in boarding school."

I took the cloth and did what I could to remove the biological material that had been left behind. "My last academy had disciplinary staff and security. I don't think people like them lasted long."

Vance smiled. "Sounds like a story to hear. Look, they aren't criminals, just forceful and a little stupid. You'll learn to get on their good side, or at least stay off their bad side. No security here to help you other than the curfew watch, and they won't step in to help, except to take you all up for a disciplinary when the dust settles. Around here, you have to learn how to handle your own."

Vance had a way of talking that was engrossing and made you want to listen and pay attention. Charisma, some people called it, and it poured from him. His word choices left me wondering where the sentence was going, and the sound of his voice was inviting without becoming snide.

"I'll do what I can," I said, keeping my answer short and simple. Saying what I knew was what had landed me here and I needed time to learn more about my surroundings and the people in them.

Vance gestured to Manson and Gil on the other side of the gym. They were presently getting physical with another student. "Some people will always look for trouble to get into. What's your story? Mid-semester transfer does raise some red flags."

Despite thinking I should keep more to myself a moment

ago, something about Vance was trustworthy. Maybe it was the open and inviting attitude or that he clearly knew more than he was letting on. The way he stepped in suggested he was opportunistic but not conniving.

This school was far different from the kind I'd previously attended. Less security, more potential enemies. Having a friend like Vance might do me some good. At the very least, I could observe and learn from him.

I gave myself another pat down with Vance's cloth and then offered it back to him.

"You should probably toss that. No reason to allow anything those two had to incubate," Vance said with a smile that I returned.

I set it aside. "I'm here because I said the wrong thing to my former headmaster," I admitted.

Vance smirked. "So Manson wasn't far off, eh?"

I bristled at that, the idea that Manson was in the same planetary system to the truth. "No. It wasn't disciplinary, more the wrong kind of help. I let him know about a teacher stealing and his wife cheating."

Vance sat upright and feigned a whistle. "Nobody likes a rat . . . what's your name?"

"Alphonse, Alphonse Malloy."

"Well, Alphonse Malloy." He paused. "We'll have to do something about that, but for now, know that people don't like uncomfortable truths. You gotta know when to leave it alone. Never tell a man his wife's cheating. That is shoot-the-messenger kinda news."

I nodded, but it was clear my acceptance wasn't enough.

"It's the principle. You tell a person something they don't know about their own lives, then you step over a boundary, right? You tell them that they don't have secrets. You start seeing through people like that and they will do anything to keep you away. Understand?" He stood up and offered his hand.

I took it and let him pull me up. "I don't know why anyone wouldn't want to know the truth. Knowing is everything."

Vance pulled me in tightly and clapped me on the back. "Alpha, we're going to have to learn that right out of you."

6

THE REST of the week went smoothly, and midway through the following week, Manson and Gil had yet to live up to their initial threat. My adjustment to the environment of Quintell Academy was outwardly easy. I attended my classes, did my work, and returned to my room. Aside from conversations with Vance, I had little social interaction.

The curriculum was no different from my previous school's. The curriculum in general was set by mandates through the Union Educational Ministry and teachers were more guides than instructors. Their synchronicity was such that the only material I missed was my day of travel.

The extended day/night cycle of Meridian was considered the human ideal. Thirty hours provided a more useful balance between activities and the sleep schedule was considered optimal for rest without falling into waste. This was also the standard schedule for those living aboard starships. My previous planet swung low at twenty-two in a cycle. A week in and I was fairly well acclimated, with several extra hours in each day to try and occupy myself.

I settled on using my newfound time to tackle the Mr. Black question. This took two forms. The first was to find a way to truthfully answer his final question, what I wanted for a future. The second was the question of Mr. Black himself. Who was he? Who did he actually work for?

I bided my time learning what I could about the school and its inner workings. First came the technical aspects of the layout. Once I had access to the academy network, it took little effort to learn the pertinent details about the buildings, their layouts, and their hours.

Most of the campus was open beyond class hours, with students encouraged to use the facilities to pursue diverse interests. The athletic buildings saw the most use, with links to the network from private rooms the next most common. The history and science buildings were limited in facilities. While the applied physics lab was open and commonly visited, the chemistry supplies were rationed only to qualified student paths.

Between brief conversations and the profiles listed on the network, it took me only half of the day to access the back end of the academy's files. Work histories, disciplinary reports, and performance reviews for each of the staff revealed nothing out of the ordinary.

The student files were accessed once I had the headmaster's information down. I learned what I could about each of the other kids I had already encountered and gathered brief details about their records in case our paths crossed. I was no hacker, but my parents had been proficient programmers and I understood the principles of informational technologies. Still, none of it had held any real interest for me. I had learned these skills because I saw the value in them as a means of self-preservation, and raw data was always a powerful weapon.

I knew that access could be monitored, so I used special access from the headmaster's account and labeled it with the name of a donor I found in the registry. I then shifted the access point to the history building. Once my digital cover was in place, I could read through files with some confidence that my actions wouldn't be immediately flagged as anything more than routine.

I went back in the files as far as twenty years prior. That was the point the academy had swapped a network protocol, which meant anything before that was beyond my reach.

There were a few references to various Mr. Blacks in the system, but none that matched the man I had met. No files referenced a Mr. Black working for Quintell. He was not a donor, a staff member, or an instructor. He didn't show up in mentions of the history or private lives of any other students or faculty members. There were some mentions through the news archives of the surrounding city, but they were nothing more than red herrings and dead ends.

My intuition told me that no such person worked for the school and that my interview in Corrin's office had been for a different purpose outside of the transfer itself.

Two questions circled in my mind, despite all of my digging. First, what was the purpose of the interview? Second, who was Mr. Black, if not a member of the school faculty?

With the trail at an impasse, I moved on to learning more about the social workings of Quintell.

Manson was my first deep dig. He had been at the academy since his twelfth year. He was transferred from a junior academy and had spent his whole life in boarding schools, and yet, according the records, his parents lived barely ten kilometers away on this very planet. Most strange, considering how most of the other children were at least a few systems removed from their home planets.

Gil's story made more sense, however. Ward of the state after he lost his father to an off-world post. His father was Union military and his mother was listed as medically unfit to parent. He had been in the boarding system since his eighth year, not unlike me.

To my surprise, Vance's file proved to be the most interesting. Vance was a deep agent from a galactic separatist unit. He was codenamed "Jack Sprat" and was proficient in all known arms and munitions. He had a confirmed kill count in the upper five figures, had escaped authorities in multiple systems, and was listed as DOA and MIA in a half dozen reports.

I found myself struggling not to laugh while reading the file. The syntax of many of the claims was off. The entire idea that he was both a deep cover agent—one that nobody was certain was alive—along with a list of his alleged accomplishments showing up in a file accessible by low-tier public administrators was ridiculous.

It was clear that Vance had accessed his own personnel file and had put in his creatively false backstory. The *why* was unimportant to me, but the *how* was something of interest. Anyone that could add to these files could also come back and read them—read any of them, for that matter. Vance probably knew quite a bit about his fellow students and faculty, the same as I now did.

I opened my own report and read through it quickly. The usual history lined up properly. Transferred in eighth year to a boarding academy, parents alive but indisposed for purposes of education and care. A note about full support from a fund set aside. Something I would have to check later.

The discrepancies started before the transfer. Listed as a severe disciplinary case from my thirteenth year. No changes to transcripts of classes or grades. Proximal reason for the transfer was special request by Headmaster Corrin.

The written report from Corrin had an interesting flaw. He mentioned a Quintell contact agreed to take me as a student. A line later, he stated a formal transfer guide was not needed. But in his closing, he left a note that the school's guide had been rude and demanding. I assumed this was in reference to Mr. Black, despite there being no mention of his name.

There were no notes left about further discipline or intervening actions. Nothing to indicate that I wasn't on track to complete my formal education within the next three years. Life at Quintell was different than before, but nothing about it was a burden.

After logging out of the network, I wrote my activity for the day in my student account. I kept the password easy to crack and reported uninteresting routine notes. Then I closed out my pad.

IT HAD NOW BEEN a full week since my arrival at Quintell, strange as it felt.

I left my room intent on heading to the athletics buildings. I would have preferred to hit the history and humanities building but needed to keep my distance after my diverted network activity.

I walked through the main entrance and headed up campus past the administration building. As I entered the cafeteria, I saw Vance heading my way. I kept walking until we were just outside the track area.

He shot me a broad grin and his signature greeting, "Alpha, my man."

It had been a week of this nickname, and despite my protests, it didn't seem to be going away. "Vance."

He saw my lack of discomfort and seized the opportunity. "Really, Alphonse? One week and you're done resisting? That shows poor form. I expected escalation, not retreat." He resumed walking, quickening the pace so I was made to follow him to keep in the conversation.

"Escalation?" I repeated.

"They must have really had you dosed heavily at your last school. Yes, escalation. How else do you establish some dominance and fight for your role in the pecking order? Constant struggle is how we young men advance the species." He adopted an exaggerated tall and straight-backed posture for this last part. His right hand clasped across his chest in salute. "We owe it to the future to be risk-taking idiots that leave cautionary tales and high-water marks."

I winced a bit at this concept of the future, a subtle gesture that the sharp-eyed Vance was quick to seize on.

"Little Billy Troublemaker doesn't like thinking of the future? More of an anarchist type, eh?" Vance shadowboxed against the sky playfully. "Take that, future generations. Alpha says you can kiss his!"

I briefly considered letting something slip from Vance's "personnel file." It wouldn't make a good escalation, as it would tell him more about my activities than his. I struggled to find something suitable. "I don't believe in futures."

Vance stopped his boxing routine and slung an arm across my shoulder. "Too nihilist, not enough rebel. You're hopeless at this."

We continued walking together across the track and stopped at a fence at the far north edge of campus.

"Not much out here," I observed. The athletic building and the humanities buildings left a blind spot to the rest of campus at this corner. A large tree blocked the southern exposure toward the faculty lodging where the on-campus staff lived.

"Good eye," Vance said. "It is about time we worked on your rebel instincts, sorely missing as they are." He closed his friendly shoulder grab into a headlock and issued a conspiratorial whisper. "We're heading into the city tonight."

I pushed Vance away, grateful that he relinquished the headlock without force. "Students aren't allowed off campus grounds without authorization."

Vance face-palmed. "Alpha, you don't hone any rebel instincts seeking permission or quoting policy. I would say you just lost any points you had, but we both know you're starting at zero."

"Look, I know you think I'm some disciplinary case from off-world, but I don't spend my time trying to upset people."

Vance smirked. "I know, Alpha, you just come by it naturally. It's what I like about you." He pointed to the fence. "We're going to sneak out."

I followed his pointing finger to the fence. There were signs of some foot traffic, but nothing particularly unusual. "I don't see anything."

Vance laughed. It was an odd sound, drifting from nervous to relief in just a few notes. "Whew. I was hoping it was hard to see, but if you didn't catch it, I think I'm going to have to wander out more often." He took a step to the fence line and started tracing his hand across the surface. He stopped at one point and fidgeted at a link for a moment. He then traced his hand around a second and third time.

I leaned in close to his back, peering carefully at each separating section of the fence. The links had been disconnected and fastened somehow. "Ah. You are passing through a partial breach in the fence that keeps from triggering the tracking system. As far as the campus network is concerned, you don't register as absent."

Vance slipped through the gap in the fence. "You got it in one. You may have noticed, but Quintell doesn't spend a lot on maintenance. They're still running software from two decades ago. As long as you don't pass any of the sensors along the top of the fence or at the gates, you're good."

I slipped through the gap in the fence and found myself with no sense of dread or hesitation in the outside world. "They must do at least cursory inspections and head counts through the night?"

Vance choked back a laugh. "Have you seen your floor manager? That lazy bum isn't doing anything, and he's pretty good at faking reports of inspections. Not that I think anyone would read them anyway." He motioned at me. "Here. Help me get the fence secured."

I held the wire and Vance made several motions like he was tying something along the links.

"Translucent thread," he explained. "A student at some

point had a stash. Almost completely invisible to scanners and no way you're seeing them with the naked eye. You can feel for them and tie them in a bow. But don't do a knot. You'll never find it again."

7

Now FREE OF the confines of the academy campus, the rest of the plan took shape.

Vance gave me a troubled look and swept me with an up-down glance. "We gotta do something about you and this uniform thing. Doesn't matter how we show up in the system if you obviously look like you don't belong in the city. If one of the teachers is out on the town and they spot us, we're done for."

"I only have uniforms," I said. The truth was I didn't even know how to get civilian, or as some of the students called them, "townie" clothing. "We can't go shopping. I don't have any money, either."

Vance snickered at that and hooked his arm back around me. "Oh, Alpha. There is so much about the world off-campus you gotta learn. Let's call this rebel lesson one. At least try to alter your appearance while we get to our next destination."

He stepped back and looked me over again. "All we really need to do for now is get rid of the blazer. Nobody walks around sporting a crest on their clothes at our age unless they are forced to."

I considered the crest on the lapel of my blazer and the garment itself. I had been wearing one for so many years, it didn't even have a weight. I slid the blazer off and tied it around my waist.

Vance rolled his eyes. "Excellent. You look like a boarding school kid pretending not to be a boarding school kid."

"No rebel points for that?" I hazarded.

Vance sighed dramatically. "We'll call that partial credit. Look, rebels don't have attachments, my man. Just ditch the thing."

I looked back at the fence and the campus. Easy enough to just leave it here. I removed my ID card from the pocket and folded up the blazer, shoving it into a depression between the outside of the fence and a clump of overgrown grass poking through to the outside. Then I took off and pocketed my tie, rolled up and pinned my sleeves, and presented myself to Vance.

He nodded. "You could still pass for a choir boy in a pinch, but at least it's not obvious where you sing the hymns. Let's get moving, we're burning daylight."

Vance pointed down the hill and into the downtown area. "All the action happens that way." Then he pointed to the west of campus and a residential area beyond. "But we're going to take a detour and find you a more permanent solution to"—he gestured at my clothes— "this."

I followed Vance for more than a kilometer as he weaved his way off the main road and into a neighborhood. Along the way, he chatted about classes and some of the different people he had seen come and go in the past few years. Quintell had more turnover than any institution he had heard of. It wasn't exactly a bad school, it just wasn't a place you went if everything was going well.

I took in the apartment buildings and street names as we moved into smaller houses and bigger yards. I found myself angry that the street names abandoned any form of pattern. They didn't stay alphabetical, so as to indicate a progression, or even keep consistent with the north/south or east/west of boulevards and avenues. Things named roads ended in cul-de-sacs, and circles joined up with terraces.

Finally, Vance stopped in front of a two-story brick façade house. It had a flat roof with angular window awnings and a porch peculiarly attached to the side of the building. "This is the place," he said.

He walked through the gate and over to the porch, bypassing the front of the house, and skipped up the three stairs with a touch of flair. Then he waved back to me. "C'mon, Alpha, get up here. Stop standing in the street like an idiot."

I followed him onto the porch and to a country-style half

doorway. The bottom half was closed and the top propped open with a rod.

Vance knocked on the door frame twice and then took a step back. Inside, the series of explosions and sudden curses stopped. A moment later, the top door was pushed open and the rod brandished by a man I recognized from the academy. It was Mr. Kurns, the facilities manager. He was in his late thirties according to his file but looked more mid-forties. He had gray at his temples along with a low fade haircut that implied military service. His file mentioned nothing of the sort, so I guessed it was more about comfort since he worked outdoors a great deal wearing a hat.

Vance gave him a hearty greeting and handshake. "Need some work done around my room."

Mr. Kurns gave me a glance and then focused on Vance. "Is he going to need some work on his place too? Haven't seen him before."

Vance nodded. "This is my main man Alpha. Only been here a week. I'm getting him settled."

Mr. Kurns sized me up. "He looks like he's never been outside. You sure about this?"

Vance nodded again and leaned against the doorframe in what I was learning was his "trust me" slouch. "You don't gotta worry about Alpha. He's harmless. Just hasn't really found his footing in this whole living thing. I'm helping him log some street smarts time." Vance handed over his student ID. "Just some pocket cash for me."

Mr. Kurns disappeared inside the house, letting the top

half of the door swing closed. The sounds of explosions and casual swearing came back for a few minutes before stopping. The door reopened and he handed Vance back his ID along with some cash. "You're low. Take it easy for a bit unless you can get a line on something."

Vance deepened his trademark slouch. "I'm good for it. I always find an angle. Now how about you check on something for my man here." He gestured at me by the door.

I stepped up and pulled out my student ID. "I think I need some pocket money and something for clothes?"

Mr. Kurns took the card and stared at Vance. "Really? Does he even know what's going on here?"

Vance gave a shrug. "Alpha, explain to Mr. Kurns what his business is for me."

It all became clear in an instant. "Mr. Kurns, as facilities manager, is in charge of ordering needed equipment to upkeep the grounds and buildings on campus. Grounds and buildings that show signs of heavy use and incomplete repair. He's ordering supplies with school funds and then misdi-recting or canceling the orders. He pockets the funds and divvies them out to students, who give him access to their support accounts. That way, he profits and keeps the school just barely presentable."

Mr. Kurns nodded. "You left out the part where I earmark portions of the student support accounts as donations for facilities. That way, the money goes to my office so I can control how it *gets spent*." He smiled with pride. "It's been a solid side business for me going on three years. I don't take on new students without a meet and greet. Looks like Vance is vouching for you. I run into trouble, though, and I have all the proof I need to show that you swiped materials from facilities."

I nodded. "That's your stratagem. You have plenty of leverage with the IDs and facilities ordering. Nobody would think twice or try to audit you, since oversight doesn't know exactly what is and isn't necessary." I paused. "So long as the grift isn't too high, of course."

Mr. Kurns smiled again. "You've got a point, Vance. This guy gets it. It takes longer for me to set up a new account. I'll move a lump sum now, give you a part, and then create a bit of an allowance for you from time to time. Makes everything nice and tidy."

"It also gives you more up front and you can always hope the student gets cold feet and doesn't return for their cash. Right?"

Mr. Kurns smiled wider. "No point in doing business if you don't corner the market, kid. Wait here." He closed the top door and again the noises resumed.

Vance took a seat and thumbed through his cash before putting it in his pocket. "You'll like Mr. Kurns, just don't try to talk to him much on campus. He has an image to uphold."

I sat down and thought about the likelihood that my parents would notice the changes to my school accounts. They didn't seem to notice, or care, that the academy name changed.

The door opened and Mr. Kurns leaned out. He looked

concerned. "Hey, Vance. Give me a minute with your friend here."

Vance shot out of his seat and gave me a broad smile. "I'll be on the road, headed back toward Quintell. Don't take too long, I'm not exactly patient. Later, Mr. Kurns."

I walked back over to the half door.

Mr. Kurns waited until Vance was clear of the side porch before saying anything. Then he pulled up a wad of bills and my ID. "You don't ask for much, do you, kid?"

I took the question as rhetorical and waited for him to continue.

"You may not know this, but every student has a personal allotment. This is money set aside by your parents to be used for incidentals, entertainment, and other things. You haven't touched a penny of yours in four years. That has me thinking you don't care to have things or you don't know it exists. So which is it?"

"I've lived on what the school provided me. I don't really care for other things."

"I'll give you some cash now, but I suggest you talk to your floor manager and get a day pass officially, go buy some townie stuff like everyone else. Otherwise, anything you pick up with what I'm giving you is going to stick out. You hear me?" He handed back the ID and gave me part of the wad.

"I'll get that set up tomorrow." I put everything in my pocket. "And this allowance?"

"You shouldn't need anything for a while unless you start

spending carelessly. Which will also be suspicious. Just play it cool. I better not see you for at least a month."

"Thank you. I better catch Vance." I walked to the street and then jogged until I caught back up with Vance. It wasn't difficult, as he had barely gone a block.

He scooped me up in his hawkish friend embrace when I got near. "You get that all settled? Good. Next, we're headed downtown. There is a clubhouse of sorts I'll introduce you to."

IT WAS JUST GETTING dark by the time we'd retraced our steps back to the academy and then into the downtown. Vance gave a rundown of our proposed itinerary.

"We'll hit the Clubhouse first. Do a quick meet and greet. I normally have a few people I need to see at these things to keep business running."

As always, he left it vague as to exactly what he was up to, for whom, and why. Vance was inscrutable at times. I wasn't able to distinguish if it was by design or that he had no real plan to uncover.

"After that, we can hit up a few other places. I know some cafes that don't look twice at students and a few stores if you want to pick up some contraband."

Contraband normally referred to items not permitted by the school code, though it was again hard to tell if Vance might also mean heavier illegal goods.

Vance stopped and patted his pockets in an odd display of forgetfulness. "Speaking of contraband, someone was expecting me to bring liquor." He looked around as if trying to make a choice on direction. "Bah. I'll get 'em next time. Let's just go."

We walked up to a corner bar with a darkened sign that read *The Clubhouse*. The windows were shuttered, and a realtor sign faded in the window. Vance pointed around the corner, then we went through an alley and around the back of the building. There, a steep staircase led to an external door. Music and conversation poured out around the seams.

Vance stopped a few stairs above the door. "Okay, look. I need to talk to some people when we get in. I want you to stand off to the side and look awkward and confused."

I knit my brow in worry at whatever plan he was hatching.

"Great, just like that. Now you just stand around and look confused and I'll talk to my people. Then we'll see what kind of action is going on. Got it?"

I frowned. "This doesn't sound like a good idea."

"I'm docking you rebel points for that." Vance went down the steps and slapped the door. The peephole darkened for a moment then opened. The sounds raged as we entered.

A guy holding a longneck bottle closed the door and sat back on his bench. He looked to be a senior or a recent graduate. The room was lit mostly with ambient light strips connected with the stereo. It pulsed and moved with the sound. The stereo dominated the south wall of the room and was flanked by two hallways. The center of the room held several couches and rough end-tables that formed a ring around the makeshift dance floor. More than a dozen students were seated and having conversations while even more spun and gyrated.

Vance left me at the door as he waved at a student on the closest couch. The two gave a makeshift hug and handshake and started talking. I could barely hear them over the music.

"I don't got it right now. I got busy and forgot," Vance said.

"I was counting on the stuff, Vance," the student replied. "My girl doesn't get frisky unless she's had something sweet and fun, y'know?"

"Don't worry, I've got some cash. Just hit up somebody here."

"Fine, hand it over. If I don't get what I want tonight, you won't get what you want tomorrow, that clear?"

Vance walked back over to me. "You can look a little less in pain and a little more excited."

"This isn't what I was expecting when you said we'd be out on the town." I found it hard to modulate my voice with the sudden drops and beats of the music.

Vance again slung his arm over my shoulder and moved me through the room and into the left hallway. "Like I said, we'll do the rounds and then be on our way."

We walked down the hall past a couple of different doorways. Sounds of engrossing activity could be heard coming from some of them. We rounded the back of the hall and into a kitchen. There, students and local girls were mixing drinks, combining the contents of a dozen bottles of liquor with another half-dozen mixers.

We passed through the kitchen and found ourselves back in the front room. "I don't see anybody I need to deal with," said Vance. "You look like you're not into the scene."

I gave a strained nod.

"Fine. There's a holo theater on 23rd and 5th. We'll hit that up."

I nodded as we reached the door and exited the clamor. "I don't think I'm rebel enough for this yet."

Vance laughed. "You can make up some points by paying for my ticket. I'm tapped out."

8

THE FINAL NOTES of the orchestral melody woven with a hit song faded out and the theater lights came on. I realized I had lost track of time and place somewhere in the wild adventure of the holo film.

Vance gave me a tap on the arm and I turned to see him beaming. "The *Adventures of Marco Grimm* kicks ass, right?"

"I have to admit, it was thrilling. The overstory of Marco as a space-traveling hunter that kills savage monsters out of alien legends was goofy."

Vance frowned and a twinkle in his eye started to fade.

I continued before it got severely diminished. "But I think the sub-plot of Marco trying to bring his girlfriend Atalasha back to life after she was cursed was surprising. And it looks like they set it up for a sequel."

Vance slugged me anyway, but his twinkle was back in full force. "What do you mean 'sequel?'"

"That charm that Atalasha was clasping that cursed her, she dropped it when Marco finished the incantation and it fell in the ashes."

Vance sat agape. "The ashes of the polar Varouth that Marco defeated to get the sixth component. Of course. That is totally going to come back to bite him in the ass."

The house lights kicked on and I saw that we were the only stragglers still in the room. "I guess we should head out."

We wound our way out of the theater. I had to shush Vance twice as we passed eager viewers on their way in. "Don't ruin it for them. That goes against the hunter's code, right?"

Vance sprang forward and hit the doors, making like he was Marco stalking a Lacona shapeshifter.

I followed him out with a touch more restraint on my enthusiasm. "That second energy drink was a bad idea, Vance."

Vance bobbed and weaved around a pair of girls heading into the theater. "No such thing as too much energy, Alpha, only a lack of imagination to use it." He slowed down and resumed his normal slouching gait as he approached me.

Too late, I saw it as a ruse and found myself back in the usual side hug of comradery he so enjoyed. I expected a snide comment about my rebel cred, but he was otherwise occupied. After pulling myself from his grip, I looked in the direction he was focused.

A student I recognized from the academy was across the street. Canton was his name. He was a ginger with pronounced freckles and the trace of a harelip scar. I'd seen him exiting the science building a few times as I entered but had no real contact with him.

Vance gave me another slug in the arm. "Hey, hang here for a minute. I've gotta talk to Canton." He didn't wait for me to agree but did give a glance back as he crossed the street. His expression implied that whatever they were meeting about would be better without my presence.

I walked to the corner of the theater near an alley and waited. The theater was to the west end of the downtown area and bordered the residential blocks. We were still far south of Mr. Kurns's place, but I couldn't help wondering how the initial city layout had been put together with such tall residential buildings here, where the downtown area thinned, and such small ones to the north where the downtown was populated with looming towers.

Vance handed something to Canton, one of the various things he hustled from one person and delivered to another for some purpose. Vance didn't offer any explanation of his activities, and I didn't ask. I wasn't sure if I wanted to work it out without help or simply respected his privacy. Neither option sounded like the whole reason.

I tried to slouch against the wall, faking my best Vance impression, when I noticed a man coming out of the alley on the opposite side. He stood out from the crowd with the fluidity of his movement, but then he quickly blended in.

After sweeping past where Vance and Canton were talking, he made his way to the corner beyond. Then he continued to follow the foot traffic and cross the street to the theater side.

I resumed my slouch and made a show of adjusting my sleeves as he came by. He had a headpiece on that was concealed between his thin hat and the popped collar of his large coat. I memorized details about the length and cut as he passed. The hat was interesting as well, the way the brim curled on the sides but looked flat from a distance.

He turned just past me and stopped to adjust a shoe as the crowd he was walking with passed on their way. I took a few steps toward the theater and tried to count out a few beats before turning back. He was gone, but I didn't spot him heading down the street.

I returned to the corner and found him making his way through the tight alley. There was a slight glow on the side of his head now. Whatever the purpose of his headset was, he had activated it. I followed along slowly, keeping my eyes on me at all times.

I followed him for a block before he turned south, then I stopped at the corner and waited again, counting out a steady ten beats before attempting to follow. I figured it was enough time to avoid any glances but fast enough to keep pace. Once I'd turned the corner, he was already at the far side of the alley.

I wasn't nervous or fearful. I didn't know what he was doing, but he didn't seem dangerous. It was more the excitement of the moment—this sense of mystery and the need to understand what this man was after. He was out here for a reason, and I intended to find out what that was, even at the risk of being found.

I waited for more than ten beats this time. If I lost him, there would be little hope to find him again without a way to track him. Getting spotted would be worse, though. He might not be dangerous, but he would certainly have questions.

I came back around the corner and saw him standing near a wall, the glow of his headset shining steadily for a nearly a minute.

I heard a window slide open next to him, and the headset light disappeared as the strange man climbed through it and into the apartment.

I didn't bother waiting this time and walked carefully toward where he had gone. A kind of rough cylinder rested on a pipe—something he'd placed here. The smell of old concession eats drifted from around the corner, and the light on the device blinked steadily. I traced the angle toward the window the man had entered.

The window was expensive and part of a linked security system. The etching on the sill indicated it was a Klemtite Essentials system, and the red light from the cylinder flashed at a point just above the sill where the window would normally sit.

I ducked under the glass window to get a better point of view. Inside, I could make out a room and a hallway beyond. A light source was on somewhere in the house and the geometry and white walls suggested it was a bathroom light bouncing from the upstairs floor. I stepped back and looked up to confirm a small sliver of light from the second story coming around the edges of a curtain.

I made my way back to the corner facing out to the street in front of the theater, waiting for the stranger to return.

After about five minutes, the man emerged from the window and closed it. He took the device with the red light and switched it off, then proceeded further down the alley. I left the corner and followed him again. This time, he didn't stop each block but continued for exactly sixteen blocks. He moved back and forth through each alley with confidence, painting a path toward what had to be his hideout or drop-off point.

I matched my pace to his as he traveled with some winds and twists further west and slightly south, until finally I came to a smaller three-story mid-rise building adjoined to several others. A sign on the courtyard gate listed it as Cascade Gardens.

He entered through the front, disappearing behind a set of foggy glass doors.

I lingered for a few minutes before realizing how long I'd been gone, so I turned around and made my way back to the theater. I came out of the alley to find Vance leaning against the very corner I had been waiting on.

Vance gave an exaggerated shiver. "Where were you, Alpha? I'm dying of cold out here worrying and waiting for you."

"It's sixty degrees," I returned. "Hardly what I would call cold."

Vance stretched and walked to the edge of the street. "Still, you were gone. I've been waiting. Where were you?"

"I took a walk." Technically it wasn't a lie, just an omission of context.

"Just a walk? I almost had time to finish a whole new snack tub." Vance gestured to an empty container jutting out of a full trash can. "Okay, I did finish one, but I was really thinking about getting another."

"I guess I can fill you in on the details if you want to let me know what you were giving to Canton."

Vance stretched and rubbed the back of his neck. "Yeah. I think I was just having a chat and you were just having a nice long late-night walk."

I grinned. "Seems like."

Vance started walking toward Quintell. "Keep this up and you might actually graduate to something beyond rebel in training."

9

I PACED IN MY ROOM. The excitement I felt tracking the man with the headset had not subsided and I found that I couldn't sit, let alone sleep.

His actions were too precise, his methods well-thought-out and assisted with cunning technology. Given his clothing and the devices he employed, the robbery itself was almost certainly not about money.

The object being taken was unlikely to be worth more than the time and equipment to take it. The fortuitous nature of the missing wire mesh from the entry window suggested both deeper pockets and a matter of influence. The object stolen was likely about power or manipulation over simple profit. And if it was, then it meant the object was priceless, which seemed doubtful considering the location.

I had tracked the man to a building but didn't have time

to see if he'd left. The building was the last thread that I had learned. It wasn't, however, the last thread I had to pull. He left several other clues, and I needed to follow each of them up to get an idea of who he was and why he acted the way he had.

It would take considerable legwork to find the right information. Network access was unlikely to get me all the pieces I needed. Fortunately, Mr. Kurns had given me an idea of how I could do this. I opened the Quintell Academy site on my pad and navigated to student services. There was a form to fill out to request a trip into town. The request needed to be filled out and the disclaimers indicated it would take several days to get approved, and still more days to arrange the actual outing.

I closed the site and reconnected the pad to show an access from the administration building. I skipped to the administrative login and entered the headmaster's credentials, then took a moment to look through the access logs for earlier in the day and found how Mr. Kurns shuffled the funds from my account to his department. It was confusing and I lost the trail. Another puzzle I would need to delve into.

I backed out and accessed my support fund account to see what Mr. Kurns had learned there. The amount open to me was not listed in a numbered amount. Instead it listed a Tertiary Inc. and the term "secured in trust." A quick network search found that this was banking code used to describe an assurance, usually given between businesses or other legal entities, to pay for any expenses based on the word of the company itself. With the name Tertiary Inc. in hand, I now had three puzzles to unravel.

For the immediate task, I dummied a form and backdated it. Then I approved it and assigned Proctor Camille Maevik to escort me to town.

I requisitioned three destinations with optional secondary stops as needed. I listed a trip to a clothing store, a tech supply store, and a job shadow tour of Klemtite Essentials.

Buzzing with the possibilities and a plan firmly in place, I let myself drift off to sleep.

───────────

For the first time I could recall, I found myself desperate for class to end. Even the dullest material provided interesting avenues for watching the reactions of other students with a lower tolerance for information absorption. Perhaps this was a manifestation of my own eagerness. I had never felt a pressing need to do something with my time.

I had also not made plans for my own reasons in the past. The final class wound to a close and I quickly made my way through the halls and to the maintenance area.

Proctor Maevik was waiting at the entrance, prompt, if not overly enthusiastic, as always. She gave me her trademark confused salute-wave. "Good to see you adjusting, Alphonse. We will be ready to leave in a moment. Mr. Kurns is bringing out our transport."

The larger roll door of the maintenance building activated and winched up into the ceiling. A van backed slowly out of the shop and pulled up alongside us. Mr. Kurns exited the vehicle and held the door for Proctor Maevik. "Sorry about the radio. Damn thing is jammed on and a bit loud. She'll get you where you're going." He nodded to me with a wink while Maevik got situated inside.

I opened the door and was startled by the loudness of the music, but I sat down and strapped in. Clearly, conversation with Maevik would have to wait until later. There was little concentrating to be done over the noise, so I nodded to her and indicated I was ready to go.

To her credit, she didn't try to speak over the sound but simply put the transport in gear and headed out. The shops I wanted to visit were already loaded into the itinerary from the forms I had put up earlier, so there was no need to discuss our next destination anyway.

We hit the road and made our way into the downtown area, but I didn't recognize the streets or the route. Driving often took paths that walking both excluded and didn't account for. As we rode, I heard subtle noises under the music. Mr. Kurns had jammed the radio himself to cover up the age and shoddy care of the vehicle. I smiled to be "in on it" and listened to the stress of the engine and shaking of the panels as we made our way east of the theater and into the far southeast corner of the downtown area.

Maevik pulled into a parking garage in the area and parked, shutting off the transport. The music ceased, leaving an intense silence that rang in our ears. "Do you think we'll need several trips?" she asked.

I considered the large amount of space in the transport. It was designed to carry full loads of students or gear for the academy. Mr. Kurns had removed the other seating and put in a variety of nets, which created pockets to organize cargo.

"I'm only buying a few essentials. I think I'll be able to carry it all in one go, Proctor Maevik."

She frowned and shuffled her scuffed shoes on the floor. "I told you, call me Cams."

"I'm not good with nicknames. It's strange to use them for school staff, so I'd rather not." I tried to sound reassuring but probably came across as condescending.

She smiled and opened her door, turning back to me before I had finished unstrapping my seat belt. "My role at the academy is as a supporter. I am not officially a teacher and I don't have a regular schedule like the rest of the staff. Think of me as an older sister. I'm here to bridge the gap between boarding school and the outside world."

I nodded and opened my own door. "I'm quite certain your job description is to monitor students for truancy and during exams. You're more *covert security* than a sister."

She came around the side of the vehicle once I was outside, then fixed me with a steady glare and an overly warm smile. "I'd like to think my security days are behind me. Can you at least try to loosen up there, Alphonse? Live a little and be a rebel every once in a while. You might find that it suits you." There was a warning in her stance. Proctor Maevik had a past that I was suddenly much more interested in learning about, but that would have to wait.

I nodded again. "I'll follow your lead, Cams," I said, giving her the satisfaction of the name. "That is, if you don't mind that I'm only a rebel in training."

She clicked the heels of her ratty shoes together and performed her salute-wave. "There are plenty of ways to get into trouble, Alphonse. Dare to be original." Her smile remained warm, but there was a haunted quality in her eyes. Something I couldn't place, but I knew without knowing that she had suffered a loss. Not just a loss, but a sacrifice.

I walked after her and we departed the parking structure onto the street. Maevik threaded through the crowd of shoppers efficiently, leaving me to sometimes apologize to a bystander or wait for a group to pass. She really knew how to get through a crowd, finding gaps and predicting the ways the lines would shift to allow her in. It was a shame she kept forgetting I was following along.

Our first stop was a mixed styles and ages clothing store. I had picked a general shop to get an idea of what I was looking at. Clothing was a diverse pursuit and creating an individual style was more important than following a trend. Or so I had read, which in itself created a kind of "look unique" trend.

I walked from aisle to aisle, reviewing the different colors and fabrics. Nothing "spoke to me" or "jumped out at me" like the fashion articles suggested. Everything looked like clothing.

Maevik watched patiently for nearly an hour while I browsed and touched nothing. "If I didn't know better, Alphonse, I would say you were just wasting time being off campus."

The accusation startled me. "I don't know what I want. Nothing seems any more useful or important than the others."

"Well, how do you see yourself? Or how do you want to present yourself to others?" She subconsciously rubbed the heel of each shoe against the toe of the other.

"Cams, you make a good point," I admitted.

Clothing had never been never about what I'd wanted to wear. It was always about how I wanted people to perceive me. More importantly, it was a way to have them *not* perceive me. My uniform had drawn the attention of Manson and Gil. My attitude had interested people like Vance and Mr. Kurns. People saw what they wanted to see.

I moved quickly then, going from aisle to aisle collecting a few shirts and pants. I picked up a few outer shirts and then some nondescript shoes. Within minutes, I had a pile of purchases. We checked out and took the bags back to the transport.

Again, Maevik led the way through the crowd with deft agility. She was also seemingly unencumbered by her bags and I fell further behind the second time. I was huffing and puffing by the time we reached our transport. Whatever sense she used to move was impossible to repeat. There were moments when she simply vanished.

We stored the load at transport and headed to my second

destination in the same area, an upscale shop that sold men's coats.

I decided to keep Maevik closer as we traveled so I could spot whatever she was seeing in crowd movement. "Thanks for the advice back there. It helped me decide what to do."

She stopped at a few gaps that appeared while she tried to focus on responding to me. "Really? It looked to me like you were just grabbing whatever. Nothing you ended up with says much of anything. It is all over the place."

I smiled inwardly but played it cool. "I thought it was best to try a lot of things. See how they felt outside of the store. Then I can make better decisions next time."

"Is that it?" She rubbed her heel against her toe again. "I better not see those clothes on any other students. Especially two I could name."

We arrived at the next store together. The pattern in her thinking and observations about crowds remained unclear, but I was learning. "Nothing like that, really. I'll show you here. I have some very specific ideas about what I need in a coat."

We entered the shop and she bristled at the sight of the displays. She pulled out her pad and checked the itinerary against the name of the shop. "I thought this was a knock-off or a junior's version. This is upscale even for boarding school brats. Uh, no offense."

A tailor was already at my elbow by the time Maevik finished her statement. "No offense taken, ma'am. We strive for excellence at Silverton's Regal." The tailor had an old-world air to him and a posture that was almost out of an anachronistic holo. "That said, sir, we will need to see some proof of payment before we proceed. Everything you see is a sample of something custom. Our clothing is made-to-order."

I walked with the tailor to the counter. He accessed his pad and I gave him the name of my student account. He opened it and nodded with approval. "Very good, sir. I'm afraid it is best if the lady stays in the front area while we get your measurements."

I looked at Maevik and she rolled her eyes. "I'll be enjoying the view outside." She left the shop and stood outside to the left of the door.

The tailor led me through the displays and into a back-room, which featured a raised platform surrounded by mirrors. "Please, sir, remove your shoes and stand comfortably with your arms out."

I did as instructed and began listing my requests as he worked. "I'm looking for a classic look. Neutral to stark black, depending on your swatches. I want it to be to my ankle with a high collar that would go above my ear when raised. It needs to have four internal pockets, two at chest level and two below the hip."

The tailor recorded his measurements. "That sounds . . . ill-fitting, sir."

I had calculated the dimensions of the coat from observations of the man and applied them to how it would hang on me. "I am buying this coat for after graduation. Your materials and workmanship have lifelong guarantees. I figured it was fine to look a little dwarfed for a year or two rather than waste your time building a coat I will grow out of in only a few years."

The tailor nodded in approval. "A proper lad. Never waste money now by thinking only short term. We will be happy to craft you a coat for a lifetime. I will draw up a design at once. Take a look at the swatches we have here, and I will be right back."

He presented me with a pad embossed with the Silverton's Regal logo then left the small measuring room and entered what was likely a studio. I quickly flipped through the swatches and located the one I recognized from the man with the headset's coat. I then left the swatch menu and scrolled to customer histories, checking against orders that used the same color. From there, I was presented with a list of only three names, two of which had the proper dimensions of the length and collar. Neither had the pockets.

I scrolled back to the swatch screen as the tailor reentered. He took the pad from me and confirmed my choice. Then he hit a few more buttons and presented me with the finalized image. "Is this to your liking, sir?"

I considered the picture for a moment. It was nearly identical to the coat worn by the man. "I think no on the collar. Half that and make it double-breasted. You never know when you might want to dress to the other side."

The tailor smiled this time. "Taste and a touch of wit. I do hope I will see you again, sir. I will have this ready in ten days. Would you prefer delivery, or will you pick it up?"

I spotted the test and waved away the offer. "I will come in again for last-minute alterations. Nobody should buy a custom garment and not have it adjusted at final purchase."

I LEFT the Silverton's Regal shop and Maevik was already ahead of me by the second step.

She turned and walked backward, still expertly dodging through the crowd while questioning me. "Care to explain that decision?"

"Graduation present," I told her. "Need something to look good for post-secondary admissions interviews." It was a good reason and plausible. I didn't feel like it was a lie, just maybe missing some more immediate pieces of relevant information. "Two more stores and then we can visit Klemtite Essentials."

Maevik spun on one foot until she was facing forward. Even so, I noticed a bit of apprehension. She clearly had a connection to Klemtite somewhere in her past.

The next store was close by. Upscale shops tended to be near each other to share the overlap of rich impulse shoppers. We entered the Daft Haberdasher and I cringed at the reference. Refined taste didn't necessarily mean good taste.

We were greeted on entry by a pair of women. One was older, with gray hair and that puffy and loose skin of the oldest workers. The other was about Maevik's age and sporting brightly dyed, close-cropped hair.

"Welcome, seekers," said the older one.

"What can we wrap around your head?" said the younger.

"I'm looking for a hat. Black in a bowler style but with a brim that turns down at the ears. Only a little. I want it to look almost flat but provide a bit of wind shielding."

The two women looked at each other. "Rather specific, young man," said the younger one.

"Seems like something you've seen before," said the older.

"Yes. It was something I saw in the past. It was worn by a man of means and distinction. I thought it might be fitting." Again, not technically a lie, just some careful wording that allowed wrong interpretations. Even so, I blushed a little as I said it.

Again, the women glanced at each other. "We do custom work here," said the older one.

"But we do have images of things we've produced before," said the younger.

They showed me a pad with a list of images, and I scrolled through until I spotted the hat the man was wearing. I needed more information than one image. "Cams, do you want a hat? On me."

The two women looked to Maevik, who swatted them back abruptly. "No. It is inappropriate for me to take gifts and I'm not into . . . this."

"Oh, c'mon. Let them get a measurement of your head, for future reference." While she overreacted and drew attention, I accessed the purchasing files from the shop's pad and found a list of names. Only one was familiar: Remington Kupfer.

I closed out the pad. "I'm sorry, ladies. I've thought about

88

it and I'm not sure I want a hat at this time. I'm picking up a coat in a week. I'll consider and stop back then."

Maevik hastily retreated from the shop and I followed her out.

"That was too much, Alphonse. I'm not here to be bribed and used as a shield. I don't know what you were doing in there, but I'm calling your day out over. Now let's get back to the transport."

I watched her sink into herself as we walked back. Several times, she made her nervous twitches with her shoes, and she also rubbed her arm a few times, the one she used to give her awkward wave/salute.

I didn't know what had happened to her, but it clearly involved Klemtite Essentials and the imperfect replacement of several of her extremities.

10

I WAITED until the next rest day to pursue the next part of my plan. After Maevik's retreat, I was unable to study the logistics at Klemtite Essentials and how their security windows could be subverted. Searching through the network only produced their boilerplate on how the windows worked. I could make some guesses as to how they could be defeated, but they would be poor at best. Their policy for repairs and replacement listed "prompt," which again gave no specific timeframe.

I did have a name and a location, so I got up early and left campus through the hole Vance had shown me before.

Invisible bows proved an upsetting challenge to untie and tie again.

It was a quiet morning. I saw only a few service people and exercisers out on my walk back to the building I had seen the man enter in Cascade Gardens. Cascade Gardens was a middle-class residential park. It was meant to house graduates and young couples starting out in life and working toward moving into larger homes or off-world careers.

Such a place would have frequent moves in and out and make a good place for shady people to operate. Their comings and goings would not be watched like a tight-knit community or overbearing monitored neighborhood. It also offered a host of amenities meant to socialize the residents and make up for the lack of privacy and overpriced rent.

I took a seat at a table in the common area. There were a few trees, and the grass was in good enough condition. I laid out a drink and a small breakfast I'd picked up on the way, then I pulled out my pad and proceeded to feign working on a paper while I waited. The long dawn had some advantages for a person like me. I was more easily tired and confused from the shift, but I could rise quickly in a world where people were used to a slower and more thorough pace.

At times I was tempted to pay attention to the pad, to ease the tedium of waiting by doing something to pass the time. This risked missing crucial information, so I took to creating a pattern of gestures that could be seen from the outside as natural. I feigned typing for a minute, moving each finger in rhythm to beat out an incomplete sentence. Then I scrolled up and down a non-existent page. Finally, I put the pad down and took a sip or a bite of food.

Each pass through the pattern, I changed the order and doubled up on some. Once the food and drink were exhausted, I took to acting like I was playing a game for a few minutes between other steps. Acting like I was playing started to take more concentration than it was worth, so I pulled up a spatial puzzle and idly solved sections between.

Distracted was distracted, but bored was bored. Mental stimulation when watching carefully was important. If I found myself doing more of this in the future, I would load up music on my pad ahead of time. Something that could be engrossing or ignored at will without moving or adjusting.

Four hours passed with nobody leaving the building the man had entered. Some entrances and exits occurred in the three other buildings that lined the courtyard. There were no above-ground connections between the buildings, so I assumed these were not important.

The door to the building opened at four hours and twelve minutes. A little girl in a blue coat and black leggings came out. Her hair was a mousy brown and she wore a headband that matched her coat. Her parents came out close behind her. Father was a blonde man near thirty. He also wore a blue coat and casual clothing. Mother emerged with him in active wear and holding a bag. She was younger and had darker hair.

The little girl pointed toward me, and the mother waved in my direction. The man grabbed the girl's hand and ferried her to the entrance of the parking garage. A minute passed and the door opened again. It was Remington Kupfer. He wore the same coat and hat but no headset. He stood at the edge of the stoop and looked out in my direction. I poked at my pad as if playing a game.

A woman exited next. She was striking in contrast to the nondescript Remington in his coat and hat. She had bright red hair—not so bright to be obviously unnatural but not so light as to be obviously natural either. She had on a long, thin white coat with thick black boots. Her eyes were a faint crystal blue, which merged with her sclera in such a way that it made her eyes appear huge at this distance. She appeared neat and refined, nothing out of place. Her nose was particularly small but strong. She wore a silver necklace with a small but noticeable diamond.

She walked to the bottom of the stoop and the man followed behind her. They headed across the courtyard and stopped behind me, then I heard a door open.

I gathered my now empty food and drink containers and tossed them in the trash, then sat at the table in the opposite direction. Moving my vantage point was risky but listening alone would limit my information gathering.

A second man had joined the pair. He was decidedly more heavy-set than Remington—both taller and more muscular. Despite his imposing physique, he had kind, almost sad eyes and was smiling broadly and easily. He gave no sense of awareness to his presence, broadly gesturing and standing at a slight tilt. He reminded me a bit of Vance in his command of lazy posture.

The three were conversing in low tones. I could make out just enough words to know what they were doing. The large man's gestures were emphatic but non-specific. The woman was close and sparing with her gestures while standing with her back to me. Remington was the most alert to outside presences and made no gestures, his arms at his side. He followed the conversation with his eyes only, glancing slightly from one speaker to the next and only offering a few words in between.

"What am I doing next?" asked the large man.

"Remi has the package," the woman replied. "So it is up to you to get it to the storage unit. The delays have been resolved. Everything from here on works like we planned."

"I don't like changes," said the heavier man.

"It's not a problem, Winston. Better to move things in stages. More time for other trails to cool." She gestured to Remi. "Let's get it done."

"Here?" Remi asked. "Shouldn't we—"

She cut him off. "We're three neighbors chatting. Just hand him the box and stop making it awkward."

Remi slid a hand into his coat and produced a box. It was easier to make out in the light of day but still impossible to determine what it was and its importance. I was sure it was the same object he had taken from the house behind the theater.

I stood up and walked toward them.

Winston took the box and slid it into his left pocket. "No more delays, then?"

The woman spread her hands wide. "No more problems. Everything works as before."

Remi saw me approaching and turned slightly, his right

hand sliding into an outside pocket. "E, there's a kid needs to get by."

The woman turned to spot me and took a step to clear a path. Winston also adjusted his position to give me passage into the building.

I stopped at the periphery. "Hello. I've been waiting for you. My name is Alphonse Malloy. I'm a student and I'm interested in what you're doing."

The woman raised a hand in warning at Remi. Winston stayed relaxed against the side of the door up on the stoop. "We're having a conversation, Alphonse."

I pointed at Remi. "That man, Remington Kupfer, took that box out of a residence behind the holo theater two days ago. He used some sophisticated tech and a prearranged gap in the security to do it. I followed him to this location. It took me a while to figure out his name and to confirm he rented here. I had to be sure this wasn't the drop-off point."

The woman laughed. "Oh, Remi, all that time and preparation, all the money sunk into accessing the house and leaving no trace and you let a child see you lift it? It would be funny if it happened to anyone, but knowing it happened to you is even better."

Remi remained expressionless but adjusted his stance to more fully face me.

The woman focused her full attention on me as well. "What else did you find out about us, sweetie?"

I smiled. "Your operation isn't about money. Or not just about money. There is a power leverage element. You also needed to arrange the repair of the Klemtite Essentials security system. I see that Winston has a jumpsuit on under his coat. He works for Klemtite, at least part time. You couldn't have stolen the uniform. It fits him too well and is too faded. A new uniform would be crisp and a stolen one wouldn't fit his large frame."

The woman's mouth slowly curved into a smile. "And Remi?"

"I noticed that his coat was well made and fit too well to be off-the-rack. I made some guesses based on the proximity of this building to the shopping center in downtown. I then tracked down people who purchased coats like his and cross-referenced it with people shopping at the nearby haberdasher."

She put her hand to her mouth to contain her laughter. "So, what do you want, then?"

It came down to that question. Since I had started on this investigation, the excitement I had felt had been building, but I didn't know why I was pursuing it, other than that it was fun. Was that all it was? Fun? No, there had to be more of a reason to it. I wasn't so childish as to pursue such a dangerous course simply for the joy of it. "I want to do a job. I want to face challenges and overcome obstacles to complete a task," I finally told her, and it was true, as much as any answer.

She could no longer contain her laughter and gave herself the satisfaction of a trill. "Why would I hire a school boy to do the work of a trained professional? Especially a child from a boarding school for feckless elites and upstart money hoarders?"

I felt my arm tense. How did she know what school I came from? I wore nothing of my uniform and had chosen my outfit to be one that would blend to this apartment's residents. I needed to direct the conversation.

I spoke quickly, establishing everything I could as fast as possible. "I've already found Remi's full name. I also know for whom he works. You trust him, but he is only an employee. He's holding a gun in his pocket. Small caliber with high-impact rounds. Polyfiber grip. It holds eight in the magazine and he has one chambered, because that's the better option. Default safety removed, but he has trigger discipline. He's ready to fire but knows it will draw attention, so it is a last resort." I took a single breath. "Winston is your brother. You have a similarity in your eye and nose structures. There's also something to the way he defers to you. You are the younger sister by at least two years. The hair color is natural but accented. The touch of rose in his eyebrows reveals the shared gene that overtook your hair."

The woman stared at me for a moment. Winston laughed, but it was obvious he didn't understand half of what I'd told them. For a moment, Remi cracked a brief smile but quickly regained his composure. I had impressed him, I knew, though it was clear to me now that I'd missed at least one detail on the gun.

"The delays in the process explain themselves," I continued. "The delay to set up the untraceable theft caused a timeline shift. This would have spooked your buyer, who you are now in a rush to impress and get back to proper standing with. This job was important, I think, and so you've agreed to do another to make up for the delay. It's small, but you need it done immediately to restore credibility. You feel short-handed to do it without undue risk."

The woman dropped her hands and Remi pulled his back out of his pocket. She reached into her own pocket and produced a cigarette, holding it while she stared at me for a long moment. Finally, she lit it and took a long drag, then exhaled.

She repeated this two more times. The smoke was stale, as if she had not exhausted her supply in some time.

She stubbed out the butt and tossed it to Winston. The large man caught it and put it in a can next to the door. "Alright, Alphonse. I'll take you up on the offer. One job. You work out and we'll see. You betray us and . . ." She gestured to Winston.

He walked down the stoop and made a show of placing his hand on my shoulder. His hand was nearly a third bigger than my head was wide.

"Winston will smother you. Or cave your face in. It really depends on how he feels in the moment."

I nodded to the large man and again at the woman. "I have no interest in betrayal." I warmed to the thought of doing the job, working out information toward a goal. "I'm excited to get started on a problem without a simple solution. I . . . I'm bored of simple."

The woman smiled again and offered a hand. "The name is Evelyn Rose. Come inside Winston's place and we'll get you up to speed." Her eyes drifted over me. "What we do can be described in many ways, sweetie, but none of them are simple."

11

THREE DAYS LATER, I paced in my room, unable to rest. The job would go down tonight, and I worked through each step in my head again. The arrival, the distribution of labor, the list of security devices, their potential placements, and how to deal with each.

The groundwork had been done. Evelyn supplied schematics for the building and a list of upgrades and changes. Winston had procured all the necessary tools to defeat the devices from Klemtite.

I marveled again at the simplicity of it. Access to high-end security technology meant needing to be able to test, disable, and repair that technology. What was infiltration if not the inverse of security?

Remi supplied the skills and grit to accomplish a job and had the training to improvise and extricate if needed. Extricate. That was his word. One of the few I had heard him say more than twice. He seemed to like the sound of it. It had a utility that I appreciated.

The target had not been given to me. Remi knew what he was looking for and I knew where it, whatever it was, would be. I understood that this job was a test run for me, but it worried me that I didn't have all the information. I felt that anything I didn't know could potentially ruin every other aspect of the plan.

I checked the time and saw I still had three hours until I had to be in position. So I started back from the top and walked through it all again.

I STOOD in the dark at the edge of a block of office buildings north of Quintell. The city wasn't laid out with the academy as a hub, but it was hard not to orient everything from the one place I truly knew.

The business district spread north of the downtown area, where more recreation and commerce occurred. The offices were flanked by restaurants and different shops offering oasis and refuge from the stress of big business. The industrial areas were all west and the residential mostly to the east. Of course, the city was a megalopolis with the outskirts forming into the next city and so on. My world was the one that existed within walking distance of the academy. If future jobs were further out, I would need assistance traveling. I didn't like the thought of being left out because of such a difficulty.

I watched as Winston pulled up to the building adjacent our target in his work transport. Officially, he was here for routine maintenance of the systems. A Union guard nodded to him and guided him into the building. The transport, full of useful tools, remained on the street, ready for our purposes.

I walked to the edge of the street and watched as Remi came from the opposite direction. We met at the side of the van opposite of the building that Winston had just entered.

Evelyn showed up last. She came out of a restaurant across the street and smoked in front of the van, still visible to anyone looking from the restaurant while we were out of sight in the shadows.

"Everything ready?" she said. Rhetorical. She didn't wait for a response. "This is an easy job. Just in and out. You have an hour. Stick to the plan."

Remi shoved a bag of tools into me and put on a harness of tools himself, his usual coat and hat left behind for this job. "I'll get it done. No different than before." He looked at me. "I do the job, you watch. Any trouble and you're on your own."

Evelyn stomped out her cigarette. "No worries, kid. We're the best." She returned to the restaurant. I could see her through the window seated with a couple of high-powered financial types. She was laughing and sharing drinks with the men.

Remi tapped me on the shoulder and pointed to the target

building. The operation was beginning, and I felt a flutter in my stomach. It wasn't excitement or illness, but it felt like something between the two. I think I was nervous. I hadn't ever gone into a situation where I didn't know how it would end up. Even the meeting with Mr. Black had been going through the motions. I knew that nothing I did in that office would change anything. But this? Everything I did for the next hour mattered to the success of the job.

I loved the feeling.

We entered the building that Winston was in the process of servicing. While he walked the guard through the procedures that would need to take place and the time frame, we entered the stairwell. It took some time to travel through the thirty-four stories of the building using the stairs. Remi took them two by two without missing a step. His endurance was not surprising nor was his impatience with me as I lumbered from flight to flight with what I realized was the bulk of the gear.

We arrived at last on the roof.

Remi spoke to me as he readied the climbing gear from the bag. "I told you these jumpsuits were useless. We go up one building and nobody looks our way. We plan a distraction and take control of the feeds. There is nothing to see."

His tone was gruff, but I got the feeling he enjoyed talking about the work. It wasn't too different from any of the teachers I'd encountered that enjoyed their jobs.

He fired a grapple line across to the roof of the target building. A few knots later and he was ready to go. He attached the gear bag first and sent it along the way. It slid across the secured cable through the night sky. He checked my harness and attached the lead. "Just don't squirm, and if you can't get it off, wait for me to get over there."

I nodded and held on to the lead. I took a step up and the next had me sailing through the air. It was an amazing moment. The feeling in my stomach grew, but I also couldn't help but smile. Despite myself, I found that I had to bite my lip not to shout in excitement.

I arrived at the opposite rooftop and released the lead easily, then I grabbed the gear bag and detached that as well. By the time I had the bag off the line and in-hand, Remi had arrived.

He gripped my shoulder and nodded. "Good start. Now stay close and hand me what I need when I need it. We're on a tight timer and I don't need you to slow us down."

Remi moved to a post at the edge of the roof. It wasn't unlike a traffic bollard. "Jigkey."

I opened the smallest of the gear bag's three compartments and handed him the oblong rectangle. He pressed it to the side of the post and moved it down slowly until he heard a click. Then he moved it laterally across until there was a second click. He pressed a button on the housing and twisted the device.

"Got the looper ready?" Remi asked.

I didn't. "One moment." I reached into the bag's second compartment and found the designated data pad and handed it to Remi.

He snatched it from me with a frown. "Anticipate what I need. You know what we're going to encounter, so act like it." He pulled on the jigkey to open a data port in the post, then attached the looper pad and activated it. It would record ten minutes of camera footage throughout our designated paths and then replay them until we disconnected it.

With the recorders dealt with, we approached the roof access door. Remi checked the latch and jamb, then nodded. "Circuit extender," he said.

I handed him a cord with a self-adhesive patch on its side. He slid the patches into the door jamb with a small blade, placing one on the upper edge of the doorframe and the other at the junction of the latch.

"Clicker," he muttered, snapping his fingers and holding his hand out impatiently.

I looked through the bag and was annoyed that I couldn't find the device. It was essential for getting through the maglocked doors by sending randomized impulses into the mechanism. It was basically a skeleton key made of magnetic fields. "It's not in the bag. I know it was packed and accounted for in Winston's inventory."

I looked back to Remi to see he had already cracked the lock and slipped through the door. He smirked at me. "Coming?"

I ducked under the circuit extender, which fooled the system into thinking that the door was still closed. Once inside, I placed down a wooden block and Remi let the door rest open on it.

We started down the stairs. Our target was on the twenty-eighth floor, so the trek would be less exhausting than the one I had already endured. Even so, the gear bag felt twice as heavy now as when I first hefted it.

Remi chided me as we made our way down. "Yeah, I tricked you, I had the clicker in my tool belt. I also have the multitool and the cutters. No reason there shouldn't be extras in the bag."

"Winston prepped the bag," I said.

He scoffed. "One, always double check anything Winston does. He's solid and trustworthy, but he's an idiot with details. Two, he's also not here. Never let a man on the outside pack your gear. They aren't the ones with their necks on the line when something goes missing, and they sure as hell aren't around when you can't find what you're looking for." He motioned to the bag. "Case in point."

I was surprised by his insight. "Right. I apologize."

He waved a hand at me. "S'okay, kid. You'll learn."

We arrived at the twenty-eighth floor. The process from the roof repeated. I handed Remi the circuit extender and he attached it. This time, I was able to observe as he worked the clicker at the lock. It wasn't exciting to see, really. All the work occurred on the magnetic spectrum. The clicker displayed a wave form and Remi manipulated dials until it pinged green and the door released. It looked almost exactly like a lock-picking mini-game.

We slipped through the door the same as before with one exception. After placing the wooden block at the bottom of the frame I also placed one at the top of the door, wedging it into the top of the jamb.

Remi watched me with interest. "You read that somewhere?"

"Exterior door should only need one. Interior might be stumbled on by security or a late-night office worker. It will take them time to remove the top jamb block. That buys us time to get out without needing to open the door again."

Remi sighed. "You forgot the part where they should be alarmed by the circuit extender. All you really did was waste time and supplies. Now let's move."

The churning in my stomach flipped up a notch. I was blowing it. I was trying to think so far ahead of the problems we could encounter, I didn't think about more obvious issues.

We made our way along the wall to the south. The room was mostly filled with cubicles, which we passed without much interest until I saw a blinking light out of place. I called out to Remi, "Halt!"

He looked at me and then in the direction I pointed. "Scrambler."

I fetched the palm-sized scrambler and put it in his hand, then he motioned me to step back.

He moved west to the cubicles and pressed himself against the side. Then he slipped into the one adjacent to the blinking and pulled himself up and over the thin material of the cubicle wall. Once he was in the correct cubicle, he pressed the scrambler to the data pad inside. The light went out.

He came back to me and handed me the scrambler. "Now, tell me what I did wrong there."

I ran the last moments through my head. "You snuck up on a device that you intended to destroy. There was no reason to hide from it. It might not have even been recording, but if it was, you would have destroyed it."

He smiled again. "No. My mistake was not just turning the damn thing off. If the pad was broadcasting live, the owner now knows something happened. Turning it off is just an interruption in feed. Don't destroy when you can disable."

We continued along the wall to a corner office. From there, we headed west. I saw a conference room and a break room. Nothing alerted me to any other danger. We entered the office at the far side with another set of circuit extenders and blocks.

That put us in the outer office and two rooms away from the target. Next, we needed to access the inner office. This required special permissions to open and couldn't be fooled by a clicker. There was no maglock to fool. The inner office was secured by a pneumatic seal.

Remi sat at the desk in the outer office and turned on the data pad, careful to angle its cameras away from us. An easy-to-guess password later and we had the administrative assistant's access. From there, we just opened the door. "Sometimes you gain access by going through the front door, right?"

I nodded. It really was easy to overthink some things.

We entered the inner office and Remi used the multitool

on his belt to open a panel behind a biometric touch pad. One snipped wire and the door to the vault opened.

We entered the vault attached to the office. Small safes were built into three of the walls, and four display cases took up the far end of the room.

Remi pointed to the one on the north wall. "That's our target."

A gun was mounted prominently inside the case. It was old, practically ancient, in good condition but clearly from another time. It was gunmetal gray, a color I realized was named after objects just like this. It had a peculiar set of notches along the grip, and the barrel also had something etched on it. The significance of these markings was lost on me. Something else to learn later.

Remi worked the multitool and had the case dismantled in moments. The lock on it was still intact on the now removed frame.

He reached for the gun and I grabbed his wrist. "Look there." I indicated a set of small metal nubs in a ring around the gun.

Remi nodded. "Good eye. Aftermarket additions. Smart woman knew to keep this off the record." He observed the sensors for a moment. "Give me the pulser and shield your eyes. "

I handed him the device and turned to face the vault entrance. I heard him click eye protection into place and then a sharp snapping noise followed.

"Alright. We got it."

I turned back to see small plumes of ozone leaking from the now destroyed sensors. I handed him the case we brought. He opened it and I saw for the first time that it was built to house a gun.

Remi handed me the case and the pulser, and I placed them in the gear bag. He looked at the removed display housing and then put it back on. "Better they wonder than learn their case is a liability."

We headed out, working cautiously but faster than our trip in. The blocks of wood were removed and the circuit extenders retrieved, and we made it easily to the stairwell.

Remi took the gear bag from me. "You've done enough. I'll lug the heavy stuff from here. Don't need you passing out on me."

I nodded, though I wasn't certain he didn't just want to have the loot with him.

"You did all right, kid. But why did you get involved with this?"

I breathed heavily as the adrenaline faded from me and the flights of stairs kept coming. "It seemed interesting. I wanted a challenge, and this offered me one."

"That's it?" he asked.

"Yes," I said, but wondered if there should be more. Like any question about the future, it gave me pause. Still, the feeling in my stomach made me realize how right the choice was. "Yes. This was what I was after."

We hit the roof and I disconnected the looper while Remi dealt with the access door.

Again, he mounted the gear bag on the wire and activated the winch to pull it across. I went next and he followed last.

He kept talking as we headed down the long flights of stairs back to the Klemtite transport.

"There's a huge market for this kind of thing out there. Collectors want them and the Union tries to snatch them up."

I considered this information. I knew that the Union had far-reaching concerns, but I hadn't realized that weapon smuggling was necessary with their military resources. "So individuals and groups both want these things? Any idea who this one will be going to?"

He chuckled, the first genuine sound I had heard out of the tight-lipped and composed operative. "Eccentric collectors, Union scientists. Lots of deep pockets that find value in the rare. I just want the pay. Doesn't matter the credo behind the buyer, just that their currency spends."

Remi spoke in a poetic tone when he discussed money. It made him almost verbose.

"This item here will get us square with the client and make a payday. That's money in our hands," he said.

I thought about his reasoning. "What do you need the money for?"

He pushed open the door and loaded the bag into the vehicle. "Kid, in this business, you don't ask for real names and you don't ask what the money's for. Trust me. And we're done here. Go back to your room. I have a feeling you'll hear from E again."

12

I WAITED four long boring days before making my way back to Cascade Gardens. Remi told me that was standard protocol after doing a job to make certain that if anything went wrong, not everyone would get caught in the cleanup. I supposed it would be harder to deal with for someone that was expecting payment or thought the others would abscond with the goods and leave them out of the cut.

For me, it was simply dull. Classes offered little interest and no challenge like those involved in planning or executing a heist. Even the thoughts of contingency plans if something did go wrong, if questions were asked of me, stopped being a distraction after the second day. I had run through all the scenarios and was satisfied I had a handle on the dire to the merely inconvenient.

Today was exciting for more than the obvious. Outside of hearing the results of the heist, I was getting my first glimpse into Evelyn's apartment. The previous job had been planned exclusively in Winston's place across the way. Remi and Evelyn both had apartments in the east building. The separation was as much about autonomy as secrecy, with none of the thieves being completely comfortable with each other. I had been in my own room since boarding school began. While I had seen the same people every day for years of classes and campus living, I had always been able to return to my own space at the end of a day.

I walked through the gates and into the park where I first met the crew. Evelyn was sitting with a hot drink and enjoying the cool air. Her gaze was into the sky and she sat placidly for some time. It was odd to see her like this; all my previous experiences saw her closely guarded. Here, she seemed almost . . . delicate? Vulnerable? Like there was something about life that didn't apply to her in that moment.

I paused, uncertain if I should interrupt her tranquility. Whatever proximity she determined for her personal space had already been breached and she fixed me with a small grin. "Alphonse, lovely day, isn't it? So perfectly clear."

I understood that countersigns were sometimes necessary in work, but this struck me as conversational over code. "Not too cold but a notable lack of heat," I hazarded.

She laughed, confirming my suspicion. "Not everything is meaningful. Sometimes we say what we mean because we mean what we say."

I sat down next to her. "I think I do better with hidden meaning. Any meaning. Everyday banter seems to be about passing time, not communication."

She laughed again. "Alphonse, if there is one thing that I hope you learn from our little interactions, it is a healthy respect for the importance of biding time and taking up space. Though, if I could glean meaning like you do, I might reconsider. Let's head inside."

I paused as she stood up. "I thought you might want to stay for a bit."

She scooped up her cup. "I prefer my quiet moments to be done alone. Two isn't silence, it is a conversation waiting to start, continue, or end." She walked up to the stoop and waved an ID chip to the scanner. There was a beep and the door opened. She paused in the doorway and waved me in.

EVELYN LED me to her apartment on the third floor. "If you're wondering, Remi's place is at the end of the hall. Easy access to the stairs and the roof. He's always been ready to leave, considers it a virtue."

She opened the door and invited me inside her one-bedroom apartment with a joint kitchen and living area. The door to the bedroom was closed. The kitchen was a cherry red color and the living area was done in creams and soft whites. There was an opulence to the décor that was further set off by the opalescent lighting.

Evelyn watched me inspecting the place. She gestured to a seat. "Please sit down and take it in. No reason to stand like an idiot. Can I get you anything?" She didn't wait for an answer before walking into the kitchen.

The kitchen was separated from the living area by an island and a low shelf, which created a small window into the area. Glassware hung from hooks in the intervening space, so that all I could really make out from movement in the kitchen was distorted shapes and morphing colors. For being an open space attached to the other room, it was surprisingly separate visually.

The place was above reproach in the cleanliness category. Not a speck of dust floated in the air. Nothing was smudged or darkened with use. The furnishings were functional but not particularly comfortable, and the seat I sat in felt stiff and ill-used. The material appeared expensive but lacked that broken-in quality. The place seemed almost clinical, if the clinic catered to an upscale clientele.

The floors were dark and looked to be either natural wood or a good re-creation. The lighting was automatic, brightening and dimming as Evelyn made her way back from the kitchen. She carried a silver- and gold-trimmed tray with a few cakes and cookies on it. She set it down and went back to the kitchen again, returning immediately with a second tray containing cups and a kettle of hot liquid.

I had brought a drink with me, almost more as a prop than a necessity. I looked at it and noticed how inferior the plastic cup seemed in the surroundings.

Evelyn sat across from me in a wing-backed chair. Modern materials but in an antique style. It gave her a commanding presence, almost like royalty.

She poured herself a cup of the liquid and one for me.

"I like to live, Alphonse. Unlike my brother, bless his simple needs, or Remi and his one-foot-out-the-door approach. A person's home is a sanctum. A place they can feel closed to the world and open to themselves."

I nodded, but I didn't understand the sentiment. I had lived in a small room at home and a series of blank spaces since. I didn't infuse my personality into my surroundings any more than I did my clothing.

Evelyn sipped her beverage and held the cup carefully in her hands without resting it on her in her lap. "Tell me, Alphonse. What do you see in me through my apartment?"

"I see that you don't live here. You spent a fair amount to upgrade the place from the stock model. The floors in particular must have been both costly and taken some effort convincing the building owner to allow it. From what I've seen of Winston's apartments, the layout is identical. Or was. You added the kitchen island and the shelving. The lack of wear indicates you spend almost no time in this room. The lock on your bedroom indicates that you find whatever is inside to be more worth protecting than out here."

She gave me an appraising look and sipped at her beverage. I hazarded a sniff and was hit by the strength of it. Some kind of herbal tea with a liqueur infused in it. I sipped it and was surprised it mostly tasted like sable berry. I continued,

"The services you just put down also show little use but a high price tag. You have gilded your cage, but you aren't certain you want to live in it. Is it a reflection of a want? You wouldn't bring clients here. It is bad business to reveal so much or to be so vulnerable."

She took another sip and then set the cup down on the silver service. "It is a want. A place that I more imagine myself in than believe in. I am far too busy planning to spend any real time here. You're so good at the little things, aren't you, Alphonse? You see through people and their actions. Nothing escapes that quick mind. "

I caught myself looking at my shoes. "I'm just explaining what I know. You asked the questions."

She smiled. "I asked what you saw reflected. You didn't 'know' any of that before a few minutes ago when you walked in. These are not hunches. You are keenly determining what pieces of information to accept and which ones to reject. It is uncanny how well that ability serves to cut through the illusions people have set forth."

I tried to sip more of the herbal tea, but the first sip left me feeling flush. "I don't know. I just see how people work. I thought it was obvious. I just assumed I was doing a bad job of hiding things. Doesn't everyone notice details? Don't they just choose to say nothing?"

Evelyn leaned forward in her wing-back chair and took a cookie between her ruby-colored fingernails. "It's like the sensor array you saw on the last job. That wasn't something

Remi was commenting on. It was something he missed. And I've known him a long time. He is meticulous. Still, that is twice now that you have outdone him. I wouldn't be surprised if that didn't breed some animosity, yes?" She concluded her statement with a crisp bite of cookie. The few crumbs that fell, she caught in her other hand and brushed back onto the tray.

I put down the herbal tea and took a cookie of my own. "I've noticed people don't like my observations. They seem angry or afraid when I state the obvious."

She sat back in the chair again, the high back casting shadows over her delicate face. "You scare them because you see through them. You take apart the artifice of their armor and leave them exposed. For civilians, that is quite uncomfortable. For operatives and thieves, it is you making their worst apprehensions come to light. We live in clouds of deceit that are supposed to protect us. Nothing seems to protect them, or us, from you, Alphonse."

I felt even more flushed. The tea didn't agree with me or Evelyn's words. Either way, I was feeling poorly.

She seemed to notice my discomfort. "You have value, Alphonse. I'm not meaning to make you feel badly. Even though you have so much natural talent, you still have much to learn about people and the world. Remi tells me you like the excitement of exploring options, of confronting challenges?"

Her crystal blue eyes twinkled as she spoke and there was

a hungry quality to her demeanor. I ate a cookie and tried to settle down. "It was exciting. During the job, I was alert for what I hadn't yet noticed, for things we didn't think of in the original plan. There was a quality to it, not the unknown but of things yet to be found. If that makes sense."

Evelyn poured herself another cup of tea. "It makes perfect sense. You need to unravel the knot, to solve the puzzle. A lot of people get frustrated by the unknown. They prefer the easy answers. We use that to our advantage in planning jobs and hiding in plain sight. Would you like to get better? To face bigger challenges?"

I took another sip of the tea and nodded. "It's why I'm here."

"Good. Good." She got up and went to her coat, then she produced a pad from a pocket and sat down again. "We have another job lined up. Let me run the details past you, we'll see what you come up with."

I sat back with my cup and took a breath to focus. "All right."

She fixed me with an easy smile and grabbed another cookie. Each time she reached out, I marveled at how light her fingers were. How precisely they gripped the treat, firm but without breaking it or causing it to shed crumbs as it moved through the air.

She spoke quickly then, reciting the details with a disdain as if they bored her. "A wealthy fellow divorced his wife. It was a messy affair with more than a few cross words and untold damage to reputations in the process. The wife moved out of the estate and left behind heirlooms linking her to old money from generations and worlds ago."

Evelyn scowled a bit as she continued. "The husband, angry and petty like men of his means tend to be, sold these heirlooms for next to nothing out of spite. Fast forward a few weeks and the happy couple reconciles." Her face flashed with even more disdain as she carefully ate her cookie. "The oldest of wealth rarely splits for long, so these things are to be expected. What isn't expected was that the new owner of the heirlooms refused to sell them back."

I nodded again in a way I realized I was doing to placate but not to understand. None of the described behavior seemed rational to me.

"Greed is a motivator, Alphonse. Never underestimate man's desire for *more*," she said, a slight curve forming on the tip of her upper lip. "Pride is also a factor, and often that pride will trump greed. It is the rock-paper-scissors of human motivation and desire. The new owner was so impressed with himself over his accomplishment that he refused to sell, even above the stated value. The pride he felt at besting his financial rival outweighed his desire for added wealth. Do you understand?"

I nodded.

She wiped her fingers off above the tray and set aside her tea, then turned the pad on. "So, we were hired to retrieve the items for half of what the new owner would have been paid for their return." She gave another upturned smile. "Tell me what you see."

She handed the pad over, and I browsed through the three pages. A floorplan of the estate, a blueprint of the surrounding utilities and access ways, and a list of vendors that supplied the estate with services and personnel. The last page was a breakdown of the plan so far with notes detailing additional insights. I handed the pad back.

Evelyn took it from me. "Trouble with the pad?" She looked concerned as she checked the screen.

"No," I answered, simply. "I reviewed the information to my satisfaction."

She didn't react, only poured herself another cup of tea. "May I?" She gestured at my cup and I nodded.

As she filled the cup, I said, "Your plan won't work." I picked up my tea and took a sip.

She leaned back in the chair, letting the shadows strike across her face and build what I assumed was an intentional intimidating appearance. "Why do you say that?"

I put the tea down and pushed it slightly away from me. "Your plan counts on being able to disable the security with your usual Klemtite Essentials tools. However, the house was retrofitted with equipment from Dynamic Security Services, which also offers off-site monitoring. They'll notice the interference and dispatch live countermeasures."

"So, what do you suggest?"

I replayed the information in my head again. "DSS uses live countermeasures, but they still have monitoring systems.

If you get someone inside the monitoring station to look the other way, through bribes or cutting them in on the take, that will delay interference. A well-placed guard can make all the difference, I would wager. Do this during the new owner's wedding anniversary next week and you can use the confusion to your advantage. He won't let his wife wear the jewels because they are a conquest more precious than she is, which will leave them isolated and an easy grab."

Evelyn turned off the pad and tossed it to another chair. "You pulled that all from the information I showed you?"

I nodded.

"Very good, Alphonse. I must say, I am impressed," she admitted. "And that is exactly how the job played out when I did it."

I reran the dates in my mind, realizing that they must have been doctored. "You already did this assignment?"

"Yes, a bit of fiction for your benefit. We did this job six weeks ago. Remi got some silly girl to look the other way at the monitoring station and we had a thirty-minute window before supervisors looked in on the unanswered alarms. The owner blamed his wife and they had quite the row. Winston walked out with the goods in a gift bag. It wasn't scanned on the way out because it would have been rude to suspect guests."

I nodded. One detail struck me as needing a follow-up, but I couldn't put it all together. "Why did you ask me to look at it if you didn't need the help?"

Evelyn stood up and cleared the trays. "You wanted a puzzle and training. This let me provide you with both."

She came back out to the room and grabbed her coat. "I have other plans for you from here."

I stood up and met her at the door. "What's the real job?"

She flashed her quirky touch of a smile. "Something so much grander, Alphonse. Something they'll tell stories about."

13

I SAW Evelyn several days later. Again, she met me outside and led me up to her apartment.

I took a seat in the same place as before and Evelyn sat across from me on another couch. She placed a pad in front of me and turned it on. "No chatter or refreshments this time, Alphonse. We're pressed for time. I need some details from you on this next puzzle and then I'm off to make some other preparations. We're looking at a corporate apartment housing a young engineer. We need to get information off her pad about a project of interest to a client."

I reviewed the information on the pad carefully. The first section was a floor plan for a corporate apartment, the next, a bio of the corporate engineer, Olivia Weng. The last was notes about the local accesses and utilities. Unlike the previous challenge, no additional notes from the crew were listed.

What struck me immediately was the layout of the apartment. It was roughly the same as the one we were sitting in. There was a bedroom and bathroom to one side and a central living area. The biggest difference was that the kitchen area was self-contained through a pair of doors. Most of the living space had cubicle-style baffles attached to create a type of office.

The personnel file on Weng expressed that she was a brilliant engineer and prodigy. She had moved through schools quickly and collected an impressive list of degrees before finishing her third decade. She was also an extreme introvert and agoraphobe. The apartment was the same one she had been living in since she had arrived on Meridian.

I turned the pad around to Evelyn and walked her through my thoughts. "This apartment has been heavily retrofitted. The separate kitchen doors and the office components were put in by the corporation she's currently working for. This means that they need to keep contaminants from the kitchen from interfering with their network hardware."

Evelyn nodded and jotted notes in the pad.

"The rest of the complex isn't too different from this place, with lines of apartments on either side as well as above and below. She's an agoraphobe, so living wedged in the middle of other apartments feels the most confined and therefore the safest. This makes infiltration difficult because all the routes in require going through a separate space."

Evelyn took a few more notes and then faced me. "We

could always rent one of the adjacent apartments. That would give us an easy route in."

I shook my head. "No, the corporation either thought of that or lucked into full occupancy. All eight adjoining places show current leases. The route in is through the service lines."

I took the pad and slid the input to the services page then traced along a particular route for the fire suppression. "This line is old, installed when the building was initially constructed, and then later removed."

I flipped back to the floor plan. "See here, the corporation put in their own high-volume fire suppression. This means the old lines connect but don't do anything. We can snake a line through and install cameras in all the previous fixtures."

Evelyn gave me her little smile. "Ah. We don't take the data out, we just record the homebody genius at work and get everything we need without lifting anything. No theft makes it easier to cover our tracks. Good work, Alphonse."

I nodded. "This will allow us to avoid running into whatever security might have changed in the other apartments. From her file, Weng is highly detail-oriented. If we entered and duplicated information, she would notice the tiniest thing out of place. Her passwords will also likely be based on esoteric knowledge and difficult formulae that would restrict access."

Evelyn closed out the pad. "Exactly. You've cracked it again." She stood up and walked to the door. "As always, I have some other work to get to. I'm sorry this was such a short test. You enjoy your week and I'll have something new for you soon."

I walked to the door, disappointed that there wasn't more to it. "Just let me know when the job is, and I'll be ready."

Evelyn kept the door closed. "Nothing you need to worry about. This is the last time I'll have the legwork done for you. So be ready to gather your own backgrounds in the future. What kind of teacher would I be if I didn't help you cover all the basics?"

She opened the door and nudged me out.

It would be six days before I heard from Evelyn again. In the interim, I went to class and studied up on the practices and overlapping market of the three big security firms operating out of Foldin City.

I had passing familiarity with Klemtite Essentials, though my physical tour of their operation had been cancelled. Their work revolved around physical security with biometrics and sensors as a specialty. The group was started in the last century as an alternative to dwindling support of Union-sponsored civil police forces. What started as a private police force became a go-to for corporate defense.

Their technology worked better and more cheaply than their competitors', but the innovation dropped off as they found themselves creating both the sword and shield of the security arms race. Klemtite's folly was trying so hard to stay ahead of its competitors, it became self-refuting.

Unable to compete in the technology sector, Dynamic Security Services rose up to offer human-backed security solutions. Their monitoring stations offered low-cost solutions to high-end problems. A computer and camera could be fooled into loops and erasure algorithms. A human was fallible, certainly, but had to be accessed to fail.

The downfall of DSS's model was in their major marketing thrust: why pay top dollar for a computer program when you could pay pennies for a human. The underpaid humans quickly felt undervalued and loyalty to the company gave way to looking the other way for the right interests at the right time. My research into DSS started to uncover some interesting insights into why all security eventually failed. The corruption didn't spread into the organization—it started at the top and broke the core below. It was clear that the pair of founders were open to the company becoming a Big Brother organization, spying on clients for the right price and influence.

The third player in the area was Chrysalis Motivations. The organization had a young pedigree and was known for its avarice and greed, which led them to radical ideologies and corner-cutting business practices. The company seemed to serve as a rebuttal to both Klemtite and DSS.

Their reaction to Klemtite was to dispense with any biometrics or electronics of any sort. They reinforced everything to require physical keys that couldn't be accessed or picked without unwieldy physical objects. The objects in question also carried radioactive isotopes that had to decay at a specific rate to be recognized by a chromatograph within the lock. The prospect of carrying around radioactive keys meant security staff with heavy lockboxes and shortened life expectancy.

They also used nuanced algorithms and artificial intelligence to stochastically monitor all systems. Any interruptions to the power or timing caused alarms and dropped bulkheads, which needed isotope keys to access. Working in a Chrysalis facility was listed as a Type 3 work hazard. That said, their largest source of failure was employee theft—workers taking whatever they felt entitled to, limited only by their security access.

My research turned increasingly cynical as the sources followed became less reputable. Secrets about security companies were suspect and whispered in dead ends on any given network. I trusted only so much of anything I read and looked forward to eliminating false information as soon as I could.

I considered my next step in this process as I again walked into the park area of Cascade Gardens. Evelyn was smoking on the stoop of her apartment and waved me over. She stubbed out the cigarette and left the remains on the ground as she opened the door. I scooped up the butt and tossed it in a receptacle by the door just as I had seen Winston do several times over the past few weeks. Evelyn smoked only when she was thinking and never cleaned up the remnants.

She didn't speak or acknowledge the behavior as we made

our way into the elevator and up to her apartment. The routine of these meetings was becoming apparent as she offered no pleasantries or social interaction until the door was closed and we were in the apartment.

She tossed me her coat rather than hanging it on the rack by the door. "Get out my pad and sit down. I'll be right back."

She went into the kitchen and came back with a glass and a tall bottle of a clear alcohol. I had the pad in hand and was in my usual spot. She took the pad from me, accessed the information she needed, and handed it back.

I took a look at the presented data as I heard her open the bottle and pour a tall drink. By the time I looked up, she had already finished the glass and was pouring a second.

The décor of the apartment was also looking less kempt. Nothing so much out of place, but the furniture no longer looked pristine. There were strands of red hair in several places, and the door to the bedroom was ajar.

Evelyn glared at me, catching my gaze. "Alphonse. Focus. The pad. What do you see?"

She hadn't asked me any specific questions or explained the purpose of the heist itself. All I had were specs on a lock. It was a prototype from Chrysalis Motivations, a type of master system that overrode the mechanisms. It was subtle, barely more than a line on a graph created by a gas chromatography readout.

"It's a lock. Or a new mechanism within Chrysalis locks,

to be precise. Do you need to know how to beat it or how to get one?"

She put down the glass and composed herself. There was relief in her voice. "So, you did some legwork. I was afraid for a moment that this would take days for you to answer." She gave a nervous laugh and stood up. "I intentionally set my apartment in disarray to distract you. To make you feel pressured to find an answer quickly, and you are a step ahead. Good. Good."

I watched her put away her coat and then shut her bedroom door. "I'll tidy up the rest after we're done here." She sat in the wingback chair and gave me smile. "Now, my dear Alphonse, how do you suggest we get the locks this prototype system has been attached to?"

I turned off the pad and placed it on the table. Chrysalis information was difficult to access. The sketchy details presented in the data pad were, I suspected, partial guesses. The readout from the gas chromatography graph corresponded to nothing. I didn't have the chemistry background to confirm it, but with nothing to compare it to, it was just a line.

"You won't find the information in the network. If you found a physical copy not attached to a door inside a facility, I would suspect it was a fake."

She leaned forward, reaching for the bottle and the empty glass. She held them in front of her but didn't refill the glass. Her posture conveyed she was nearly daring me to force her to drink.

"Your best hope to find the real information is to find someone inside Chrysalis. Not someone on the design team or the security staff. These would both be trained to lie or mislead. You need someone with something to gain, someone that can be bought because they exist to be bought."

She smiled and put the glass and bottle down again. "You're describing a corporate headhunter. Someone employed to find talented individuals in a company and lure them from one company to another. Rather than break in and find the information, we just need to lure the information to us. Excellent work, Alphonse. I hope you are getting as much from this training as I promised."

I stood up and approached the door. "Until next week, then?"

She stayed in the chair, her gaze switching between the pad and the bottle. She seemed to snap out of it for a moment and turned to me. "Yes, next week. I'll have something even more difficult then. Keep up on your studies. You never know when you'll be put on the spot." She gave me her quirky corner smile, and for the first time since I'd seen her on the stoop, she seemed her usual self.

"I'll do what I can." I closed the door and headed back to Quintell.

I SPENT the next two days looking into more information on Chrysalis. Word in the network dead ends suggested they had a new type of lock in development. Something that was both more secure than their previous models and prevented the problems of their previous lockdowns. Something that coordinated the algorithms and the key isotopes.

The information I found made no sense. And it was also contradictory, with one source saying the key was improved and the next saying the algorithm was the subject of change. Conspiracies of alien technology and even mind-control implants wove their way through these discussions, casting a shadow of doubt over all of it.

One discussion mentioned a hunt for talented individuals with knowledge in both programming and radiometry. The dates were all over the place. Perhaps this was the example that Evelyn had used to create the puzzle?

Late on the second day, I found a message requesting another meeting. It came in too late for me to leave campus. The next day crawled by as I struggled to stay engaged in classes, wondering what Evelyn would have for me. Not just the puzzle itself, but what odd contrivance she would put around it in an attempt to increase the difficulty.

Vance caught me in the hallway after class. "Hey, Alpha, you got a moment to talk?"

I brushed past him on the way to my room. "Not right now. I have to get on a project. Catch me tomorrow?"

He slid into his usual slouch. "No problem, my man. Catch me when you can."

I went to my room to change and rushed to the meeting.

EVELYN MET me at the gate and walked me to the apartment, her nature jovial and a touch flirty. "Good to see you again, Alphonse. This will be a quick one. I would be very surprised if you could answer the puzzle just from what I will present."

We entered the apartment and she sat me in the usual spot. This time she sat next to me on the sofa and showed me the pad. She held it and waited for me to instruct her to move through the information.

First was a floor plan for a fabrication plant. I observed the ingress and exits and the workflow passages of the business itself. "Next, please."

She flipped to the second page, which was a list of technical specs for some type of container. There was a time stamp attached, giving a date for the day after tomorrow. "Any more?"

She shut off the pad. "No, that's all you get."

"The date was listed for two days from now. Is this real or another job you've already completed?"

She laughed at the question and faced me. The space between us on the sofa was small and her behavior was overly familiar.

"Is this part of your training regime?"

She smirked. "There will always be another challenge to face, Alphonse. Always a different set of conditions to distract. You're a bright boy. I'm sure you see right through it." She stood up. "So, let me know when you have an answer.

Message me and I'll send Winston over to the school to hear it from you. He's due to complete an inspection on the grounds this week."

I got up and walked to the door. "What is it that I'm doing? What do you need solved?"

She paused with her hand at the door. "Oh, silly me. How would you get that container out of the factory?"

I considered for a moment. "I'll give you an answer soon."

"Of that, dear Alphonse, I have no doubt."

I worked on the issue for the rest of the evening and into the next day. The fabrication plant was a tight operation. They manufactured state-of-the-art containment vessels. Each was custom-made to exact specifications and the plans only existed until the job was done.

I suspected this was to prevent duplication, so it would be unfeasible to get a copy of the vessel. The only real solution was to get the one being made, which meant that the theft would be immediately noticeable.

I looked at the fabrication plant's order and request procedures through the network. They offered final moment changes and adjustments to ensure the utmost quality. That was the key.

I walked around the grounds and found Winston talking to Mr. Kurns at the maintenance building, so I went up to the pair. "Hello, Mr. Kurns. Doing some security changes?"

He shook his head. "Just a routine look around, nothing serious. Anyway, we're done here. Don't get in the inspector's way, Alphonse."

Mr. Kurns went into the maintenance building and I walked behind Winston's van. He followed after a moment. "E said you would tell me something?"

I looked around to see that no students were looking in our direction. None of them seemed the least bit interested in the security inspector and his van. "The update protocol is the key. Send a change of address within ten seconds of the completed fabrication and the factory won't know anything has changed for days."

Winston gave me a broad, toothy smile and slapped me in the arm with his almost comically large hand. "I'll let E know you told me. She'll want to talk to you again real soon."

14

ON THE SECOND day of Winston's inspection, he passed me a message from Evelyn. It was simple but conveyed a sense of her personality.

> *Time for more outside training. Homework and legwork go together. Meet*
> *Remi uptown for a night out to remember. PS. Bring drinks and mittens.*
> *– E*

The message was both instructional and a code. The references to drinks represented a bar in the uptown area. The mittens reference wasn't about the name but what the bar offered. There was a sub-zero bar called McCool's just off Park Street, which was a clever use of the postscript. The reference to time and the repetition of "out" meant two o'clock.

It was the night before rest day, so I was glad I wouldn't have to pull double duty the next afternoon if it went long. I made my way through the streets and to the appointed building. I'd considered showing up early, but a time had been given for a reason, so I decided to wait until then and follow instructions.

At exactly two o'clock, the door at the side of the bar opened and Remi poked his head out. "Get in," he told me.

I moved from the corner to the door quickly but fluidly, as Remi had instructed in our gun heist.

He nodded as I approached, reinforcing the earlier lesson. "No matter how fast or slow you move, if you do so consistently people will assume you have a reason to be there and won't be suspicious," he reiterated.

We stood in a stairwell linking the back end of the bar with a series of utility tunnels that dipped below the refrigeration systems.

He looked over my outfit and scowled. "Really? In matching coats?" he asked.

"It was the only thing I had that seemed appropriate for a night mission. I wasn't given any specifics," I said.

He sighed. "I would say it was a bad idea, but that is hypocritical. Reason I have the coat is it blends well with night work. Just don't ever get yourself a matching hat."

After walking up the stairs and into a position on a sub roof, we were below the bulk of the commercial building, which went up another fifteen stories but was still below the signage for McCool's. Remi had two sets of field glasses set up just above the protraction of wall below the sign. From the street level, it would be almost impossible to make us out against the glare of the sign and the shadows of the sub-roof.

We took up position at the glasses. "You take the pad and jot down everything you notice about the people coming and going from the building across the way," said Remi. "I know you like to rely on your memory, but we need the data. Observe, write. That's your job. Got it?"

I took up the pad and glanced through the glasses. The building across the way was a simple four-story structure. There was door facing our direction and lights on across all four floors. Connected to the south side was a parking ramp that led underground. "What am I looking at?"

Remi chuckled. "Hard to know what something is that doesn't give itself away, huh? No information means you have to know what you're seeing to see it. That's a shift change station for the Union forces in the area. Private security handles most of the policing and guard work for Foldin City but it's still a Union colony on a Union world. That means they have to maintain a presence. They just keep it under wraps."

"Do I count cars, or do you have a plan to get more information from them than I know about?"

"Glad you are already up to speed, kid. Hit that button on the field glasses and it will show infrared. That won't give you a complete view, but it will let you count bodies. Any other questions?"

I surveyed our immediate area. Aside from the pad and

the glasses, there was a plastic box. "What's with that?" I asked, pointing to it.

"Drinks and snacks. We're going to be up here for a while, so get comfortable and stay focused."

I stretched and resumed my position at the glasses. "Is that until first light?"

"You'll know when we're done. Now test the infrared. Get used to the view and be prepared to swap back and forth quickly. If you have to adjust, you'll lose valuable data."

I checked the setting and worked it back and forth. It was difficult to make out anything from the changeover at first. The colors blended into each other and the brightness overall made swapping back to regular vision difficult in the dark. After a few adjustments, I concluded I was basically ready. "I'm set."

We stood in silence for a few hours. I wrote down everything I saw from the people entering the building and the number of transports and passengers leaving. The comings and goings were sporadic. For an hour, nothing would happen, and then there would be a rush of arrivals for nearly twenty minutes. Then a pause and several transports would leave. No transports entered in the hours I watched, and nobody walked out of the door, only in.

It was strange, but I knew I lacked perspective to understand what was happening. I continued to watch and tried not to consider the implications until I had more to go on.

Remi observed as well, quietly taking his own notes. He

would periodically inform me that he was "taking a lap" and I would be left alone to record.

When he returned, he said, "You don't ask many questions."

I kept watch through the glasses. "You explained what I was doing. If I need something more, I will let you know."

"Not what I meant, kid. It isn't a question, it's an observation. There are people that ask questions constantly, people that don't know what is happening and try to solve the problem by demanding to be told what's what. Then there are the people that wait quietly, gathering information, and then announce what is happening. It isn't always quite that simple, but those are the general groups. Too often, the people that ask questions don't think enough. They are frightened by silence and being forced to do their own work. They want the real trials to be complete and to reap the rewards without effort. Those people can't be trusted. You hear me, kid? Don't trust someone that doesn't do their own legwork."

"That makes sense."

"Now the other side," he continued, "the ones that wait and watch and never question, they have their own problems. That means you, kid."

There was a pause that sounded like he expected me to fill in something. "Alright," I said after a long pause.

He chuckled. "Like that. You waited for more information, unwilling to offend to cut to the chase. You have the opposite problem: you don't care enough about the outcome to try and influence it. That's dangerous. You have to live life.

Living is about exerting your wants onto the world and expecting it to fight back."

"I don't know what I want out of life."

He sighed and then chuckled. I heard the cooler open and he tapped me on the arm, then I looked away from the glasses for a moment to accept the drink he offered. It was a thick liquid that tasted bitter. "What's this?"

"Good question. Better question would have been to ask before you drank it. But if I wanted to poison you, I would have lied before same as after. This is a protein energy sludge. I make it myself. A bit of caffeine, some vitamins, some vegetable extracts. It will keep you alert for hours. Just sip it or you'll get jittery."

I heard the sound of paper opening and the cooler closing. "You mentioned on the roof that you were interested in the in-the-moment excitement of chance and possibility. Sounds to me like you don't know what you want because you want something that doesn't have a simple label."

I considered the explanation but rejected it. That was more an excuse than a real answer. "Maybe," I said.

Remi scoffed. "Maybe? Don't kiss my ass, kid. If I'm wrong, say so. You keep placating and you'll find yourself doing anything not to rock the boat. Same as the not asking questions, a passive life is a life not lived. Act or quit. Don't just accept."

It struck me that he wasn't speaking to me, but at me and around me. "Do you believe that, or do you just want to?"

Another chuckle. "Here. Eat this if you get hungry." He

tossed a paper-wrapped sandwich onto the ledge next to me. "I'll let you answer that question for me. I used to think a lot of things that I probably no longer believe. I had a kid once. A family. When you have people who depend on you, life changes. When you lose those people, it changes again. How you feel in each moment is a shade of its own truth, but a man's mindset can change on a dime."

I jotted down a few more entries. "Doesn't that make the truth subjective?"

"I suppose it does," he admitted. "You make the world you live in. I was a Renegade before I came here," he finally told me. "I wanted to live free, the same as most who find their way to the Deadlands. That was all before I got myself trapped on this rock without a ship to call my own. Used to have one called *the Serpent's Bow*, but she's sitting on a moon in pieces far from here, probably salvaged by a crew of folks just like me. You asked me before why I needed the money. I mean to find myself a ship and resume my scoundrel ways."

"You're doing all of this so you can be a criminal again?" I asked.

He scoffed. "The fact that you only heard the Renegade part of that speaks volumes on the lack of education you received in that school," he said. "Being a Renegade isn't just about stealing and smuggling. It's about freedom. Once you have it, you can't imagine a life without, and you'll do whatever it takes to get it back."

I DIDN'T FEEL TOO tired. The conversation had been interesting. Remi didn't come across as the sharing type. Maybe he just wanted to fill the silence. The home-brew drink of his might have contributed, but I couldn't be certain there either. Most likely it was the puzzle, working out what I was seeing. Too much information and not enough significance spun me up.

I heard a sound and turned. The man walking up behind me was not Remi. He wore a nondescript uniform with no insignia, not unlike the types I had seen entering the Union building all night. He held a gun and was on his radio. "Some kid's up here. I'll bring him in." He gestured with the gun. "Move slow, boy. You're trespassing. I don't know who put you up to this, but we're going to go have a chat."

This was unexpected, to say the least. "Easy," I said, slowly lifting my hands.

I moved carefully, putting the data pad on the ground and stepping out of the glaring light of the sign. The man was wearing armor under his plain-colored jumpsuit. It hummed with power. Whatever his normal job was, arresting a kid seemed well below his usual role.

"I'm just watching people for school." I tried to sound confused.

He sneered and tossed a pair of cuffs on the roof in front of me. "You're not much of a liar. Put those on."

I leaned down to collect the cuffs when I saw Remi come around the corner from his most recent patrol. Before I could react, he had his gun ready and aimed at the guard. His eyes narrowed as his finger bent around the trigger and squeezed.

A round tore into the man's back, causing him to stagger forward, toppling, and I retreated.

He tried to turn but the bullet had shattered something inside his abdomen, and he could barely move.

Remi ran up and pointed the gun in his face.

"W-Wait a second," the man begged.

Remi didn't hesitate, and I watched the second bullet tear through the guard's skull, scattering brains on the concrete beneath him, his eyes rolling as his mouth dropped.

My throat closed up as the blood hit me, spattering across my shirt. Remi looked up at me. "Grab the gear," he said, no hesitation in his voice. "We've got to move."

15

I FLOATED through the first half of the next school week, lost in my own head.

Watching Remi kill a man had sent chills through me that I simply couldn't shake. I had watched him take a life, and all I could do was stand there.

So much of what we had done was for a practical purpose —moving wealth from one rich corporate elite to another. It was a game with loose rules and no real consequences. The death of the guard and the implications of it were all so very sobering.

I also had an inkling that more was going on than I was being told. The job of watching the Union guard station made little sense. I hadn't come to any specific conclusions (yet), but when we dropped off the data with Evelyn, she was quite pleased. She also ignored the comments about the dead guard, chalking it up as "an unfortunate part of the work."

Vance and I ran on the track outside of the athletics building near the damaged fence. It was getting warm outside and we had taken to jogging after classes when I didn't need to sneak off. This routine provided us with an excuse for being in the area if we were spotted entering or leaving through the fence.

"Hey, Alpha, get your head out of your ass," said Vance. "You almost went right off the track and into the bushes." He grinned broadly and turned around to jog backward, easily keeping pace with me as I struggled to remember to breathe and pace myself. His longer frame gave him an easy advantage for this sort of thing.

"A lot on my mind is all." I tried to smile but was too winded to fake it.

Vance turned around again and matched my pace. "Let's walk a lap or two. You need to get it together before you have me fetching Maevik or a doctor or something."

I tried to laugh it off, but I was breathing harder with each pace. We slowed past a walk to an idle shuffle.

Vance slapped me on the back and sent me into a coughing fit. He laughed at that. "Seriously, Alpha, you gotta keep in shape or all this thinking you do is going to land you nowhere. No point in living if you aren't living. Know what I mean?"

I watched the gangly Vance hop from foot to foot, energy exuding from his every action, and considered his words. So similar to those spoken by Remi but with such a different emphasis. For Vance, life was an adventure in which he did what he wanted because he could. For Remi, it was a challenge, proving he could defy power and get away with it. The same coin, but one side made of hope and the other anger.

I lay down on the grass outside of the track. I wasn't catching my breath and seemed to be hyperventilating. I thought I was having a panic attack.

Vance watched me go down and laughed. "Calm down, my man. Breathe into your hands and stop thinking."

I did as he suggested, breathing a few puffs into my hands and then a few into the air. It didn't take long for my heart to stop racing and the world to stop spinning.

Vance loomed over me while I recovered, beaming that smile and slouching against the sky. I sat up and saw Gil and Manson heading across the track toward us. They looked nervous.

Manson stepped forward, his demeanor toward me cool, but no longer with the antagonizing quality of our first meeting. Gil stopped a pace behind, doing his best to use the wider kid as a kind of shield. Gil looked like he was about to scream or throw a punch, but he said nothing and didn't look my way, just stared with frustration at Vance.

Vance sat down next to me and tilted his head to look up at the two. "What's going on? Spill it."

Manson rubbed his bare arm with his other hand. Between his posture and his behavior, whatever brought them here was bad news. Vance tried to remain calm, but I could see him digging into the grass with one hand even as he waved the other one around nonchalantly.

"We just heard them talking. The teachers to Headmaster Whiles. They say they got proof you've been swiping answer sheets and selling tests."

"I heard that Canton turned you in because he was in trouble," Gil said.

Manson stepped back, shoving his weight into Gil. "Don't bring that into it." He turned his focus back to Vance. "They said Canton might be involved. I don't know it. I say don't accuse nobody if you don't know."

Vance stretched languidly and stared into the sky. "You say they have proof?"

Gil chimed in again, this time with his hands up to guard against any more sudden body checks from Manson. "They say that a bunch of students confessed to cheating." He paused. "But not us. We'd never say. You don't cheat and snitch. That's just the long way to fail."

I knew that Vance had been dealing in information. The accusation at Canton made sense. Their meeting at the theater didn't look like everything was smooth. Clearly Canton had leverage and was trying to use it against Vance. Which meant there was something Canton knew that I needed to find out.

Vance sat back up. "It'll blow over. These things happen. Fingers point and everyone yells, and in the end, the teachers have to save face. They think they're so clever and watch everyone so carefully. Cheating's just a different way to learn.

Not like they know anything, with static curriculum and classes that could be taught by a robot." He made it sound like a joke, but he was angry.

I got to my feet. "We'll figure something out, Vance. We'll find a way to deal with Canton or Headmaster Whiles. They can't just throw you out." I said it like I meant it. I wanted to mean it. But I knew the rule and that they could absolutely toss him. After all, my last school had thrown me away, and I hadn't even broken any regulations.

Still, I wouldn't let this stand.

Vance remained seated with an unconcerned smile, staring into the sky. "Everything will be fine, guys. I always find a way to land on my feet."

DESPITE VANCE'S ASSURANCES, I wanted to get my own plan into action. To this end, I started following Headmaster Whiles. I already had access to his personnel files and password. I had been using those for my own purposes for months now, but the files didn't reveal anything that could help Vance. Professionally, the headmaster was a dedicated administrator. He was fair with employees, even when they faced scandals, and he had multiple commendations for resolving student conflicts that led to graduation and fulfilling after-education career placements.

I left campus and took a transport to Whiles' neighborhood. I scouted the area with a few passes of the houses on each side, careful not to cross directly by the house without at least one building between me and the target. Remi called it the rule of separation, that the only time you directly interface with a target is during a job. Recon was done ideally with three separations, but one would do if things were urgent.

I found a house in the neighborhood to the east of his that was vacant. The yard was kept up, but only so far, and the building was clean but sterile. I took a lattice to the roof and then climbed into an open window, then I stood inside an empty bedroom and watched Whiles' home with field glasses I had picked up. I had been building my own kit of tools but limited my purchases to things a student could be caught with or expected to have a use for. This gave me an adequate supply, but nothing as high quality or advanced as Remi's.

Whiles had dinner with his wife and two children, and he played games with the kids afterward. He later browsed something on a personal pad and sat quietly in a home office. Nothing suggested malfeasance, though it was hard to tell what he was accessing on the pad. I would need to get into his access records, but that would have to wait.

I returned to campus to dig through his access logs and financials.

The access logs revealed he was looking through the regulations on expulsions. A bad sign for Vance. Though I had to admit, it was good to see him reviewing the information and not making a move first. It fit the character I had already seen in Whiles, a fair man that worked hard but wasn't overly intelligent or creative. He had passion and dedication for his job but possessed a dull wit.

He had pulled up the backgrounds on eight other students in addition to Vance. I noted Manson but not Gil. Canton's file had been accessed twice in the day. My file was not touched. I took that as absence of evidence and drew no further conclusion. In addition, he had looked into the files and grading reports of six teachers. Two of these, Parker and Nolans, had bad records with grading policies. Their files carried more than a few reprimands for grade fixing. Whiles' own notations suggested firing and replacement, but a teachers' coalition had given them clemency.

His financials were a dull and consistent flow of bills paid, salary earned, and occasional luxuries purchased or engaged in. No sudden infusions of cash or strange splurges. Of course, the financial records could be tampered with or he could be running an off-account strategy. If Mr. Kurns's enterprise had taught me anything, it was that financial records only told a part of a financial story.

I considered the case of Mr. Kurns. Revealing his operations could be used as leverage, to show that Whiles didn't know what was going on in his own school, discrediting him as an administrator. I was reluctant to burn Mr. Kurns. He had shown nothing but support for the students. He also had information on my off-campus activities, which could be a problem. Lastly, Vance liked Mr. Kurns, so he wouldn't likely accept solving his problem in that fashion.

Canton was a piece of work. His file read like the gilded

prince of a foreign land. His family was corporate and connected. He had several infractions—ones that looked far worse than selling tests and answers—in his files. He had been caught in an off-campus incident that left another student in a coma, and he had been caught with controlled substances on campus and even turned over to local authorities. Those records had also been suppressed. Canton deserved something bad to happen to him but existed in a protective bubble. I would have to consider changing that another way.

I turned in for the night, planning to follow Whiles carefully and spot anything in his routine that could suggest his life was different than it appeared in records. From my readings of the school procedures, an investigation into the removal of a student took three days from the submission of the complaint. With one gone, I needed to make tomorrow count.

THE MOMENT CLASSES WERE OVER, I was at the gate and ready to track Headmaster Whiles, having given myself a medical release that would let me take a bus from the grounds to a specific facility. I ordered tests with a doctor that hadn't started yet but was listed on the staff, so I could explain the whole thing away as miscommunication. It gave me several hours of excuse.

Whiles traveled light, taking the same public transport each day. I sat in front of him on the bus to avoid a conversation that could crop up from walking past him. I was able to keep tabs on his position through reflections in the glass. The clinic I had chosen for my excuse was beyond his neighborhood stop.

We traveled through town with many people getting on and off the transport. The stops moved along quickly—the Union kept the transports on time, after all. I felt a surge of excitement as I carefully surveilled Whiles. This was just like the gun heist except that I felt more involved. Maybe it was because it was my plan from top to bottom. Maybe it was because I was doing it for Vance and not the thrill. I didn't have time to separate the sensations.

The bus arrived at Whiles' normal stop. He remained on board.

I felt a jolt of encouragement. This would reveal new information. In my mind's eye, I saw this becoming the smoking gun that could save Vance. Minutes later, I felt that jolt evaporate as my own stop came up. I exited the bus without looking back and took two steps into the clinic before heading back out. I crossed the street, keeping an even pace, like Remi had shown me.

The bus continued forward. I had memorized the route the night before. I knew there were three more stops before it turned and came back through. Whiles could get off at any of them. I ran through the particular buildings adjoining each. A market, which could be for regular shopping or something else. Stop two was a corporate apartment complex. Another place where illicit behavior might occur. The third and final stop . . . My heart sank. It was the stop next to his wife's employer.

I retraced my steps back to the clinic and entered. I provided my name and was told that the appointment was in error, as I had planned. With my cover in place, I waited for the bus to return. I boarded and saw Vance's hopes disappear. Whiles was seated with his wife. They both got off at their usual stop and I rode the bus sullenly back to Quintell.

I HAD FAILED to find anything that could help Vance. Any plan to discredit Canton would take too long to put in place.

I met with Vance in his room to deliver the news. "I can't find a way around it. They have what they need to proceed with your removal. Headmaster Whiles did what he could, but there's enough evidence and some teachers, and students, really want you gone."

Vance leaned against the wall, giving me an easy smile and a shrug. "These things happen."

I felt a tinge of anger. "Don't you care? Don't you want to stop this?" I could feel myself shaking.

Vance walked over and sat on the couch with me, his usual nonchalance momentarily gone, but even as he leveled with me, he remained strangely upbeat. "This isn't my first removal. I've still got two years, so it probably won't be my last."

I wanted to explain to him the lengths I had gone to try

and help. The powerlessness I felt that nothing I knew could change the outcome. Nothing except for the dirt on Canton. "Look, Vance, you should know that Ca—"

He smacked me in the arm and stood up. There was pain in his eyes. "No! Don't tell me. It doesn't matter who or why. I didn't cover my bases and things went bad. It happens, that's the risk. You trying to fix it just makes it worse. Okay? Can't you just . . . be a friend and not do whatever it is you're thinking of—"

He didn't finish the thought. He didn't get a chance. The door opened and Maevik came in.

She nodded to me and then addressed Vance. "The decision came down. I'm to take you to the transport."

I was shocked. "Tomorrow. The decision comes in tomorrow?" I asked it as a question because I wanted it to be true, but I knew then that it wasn't. Vance had known about the accusations the day before Manson and Gil stumbled onto it. His three days were up.

Vance punched me on the arm again and opened a drawer. He pulled out a small packed bag and followed Maevik out. I followed him through the hall and out to the courtyard, my mind working overtime for a solution to this— for a way to let him stay. I didn't want the only friend I had in this place to disappear.

"I can fix this," I said, ignoring what he'd said to me only a few moments ago.

Vance looked at me, setting his bag down beside the transport's hatch. "What?"

"I can figure this out, Vance. I know I can."

He just smiled at me. "You probably could, Alpha. You're the smartest guy I know, but seriously, let this one go," he said, no hint of distress. "Just do me a favor, alright?"

I nodded. "What is it?"

"When we're free of all these rules and schools, look me up," he said. "Or I'll find you. Either way, let's catch up. I wanna hear about whatever trouble you find yourself getting into."

"Trouble?" I asked.

He chuckled. "You think I don't know you're up to something, Alpha? You might be the smartest guy in the room, but I'm not blind." He gave me a quick wink. "Just be careful, whatever you're up to."

"Right," I said, almost whispering the word, and then for the first time in a while, I felt a strange fear in my throat and a growing uncertainty about what would come next. "Everyone else here is boring," I said, not quite knowing why I was saying it.

"That's the truth if ever I heard it," said Vance. "But you'll be fine without me. You're a full-on rebel now, Alpha." He opened the door and tossed his bag inside then turned back to me. I could feel more eyes emerging from the rooms and staring through the windows.

Manson and Gil flanked me, for once dropping their affectations and just standing there like wounded and hurt kids.

Vance gave us a smile. "You boys take care," he said,

getting inside the vehicle. "Catch you on the other side, Alpha."

The door shut as he said the last word, and then the engine roared to life.

Gil and Manson stood with me for a while, even after the shuttle left. We didn't speak as the rest of the crowd dispersed and went about their days.

I wasn't sure how to feel about any of this. Vance had been my only real friend at this place. I had a few acquaintances, sure, but no one else. Not like him. It was confusing, but I decided to push it out of my head for now.

I had other things to worry about.

16

I DECIDED to reach out to Evelyn, rather than wait for her to contact me. Much to my delight, she had a new puzzle ready for me to solve. I took my usual trip out to Cascade Gardens on auto-pilot. Normally, I was careful to avoid being seen by anyone that might have a connection with the academy or could be overly attentive. Today, I merely walked the streets without caring who saw me.

I wanted to chastise myself for the lack of conviction and caution, but it didn't register. If anything, I felt that the world didn't value effort. That I would escape harm just because or succumb to it no matter what. No matter how much I planned, there was always a level of chance involved.

Vance had disappeared forever, and it had happened despite my efforts. I hated myself for not being fast enough, for not being smart enough to fix it.

Evelyn was waiting at the gate to the park. She seemed at ease but certainly focused her attention on me from a distance. I must have been a spectacle the way I slumped through the street and into the Gardens complex. If she noticed my mood, she didn't comment as we entered the building and her apartment proper.

I took my usual seat and was grateful that Evelyn took a moment to pause at the kitchen rather than throwing the data pad at me immediately. I lost track of time for a moment and she was already back in the living area with a tray of hot liquids.

"Alphonse? You look like you could use some bolstering. I know these puzzles have been difficult so far, but I assumed you had more grit than this."

I looked at her, sitting across from me on the other sofa. I couldn't determine by her face if she had genuine concern or was afraid a toy was broken.

"Is this about that guard Remi had to deal with? Cost of business, you understand."

I took the offered drink and breathed the vapor, steeling myself to deal with the coming tirade. For a moment, I perked up but hid it. People had an interesting tendency to run at the mouth when they saw someone feeling pitiful. Something to remember for another time.

"I need you in top form for this next puzzle. Tell me what you need, and I'll see what I can do. Do you need to come back tomorrow? I would prefer sooner to later, but it will keep."

I considered the urgency she expressed and the veneer of concern. The more I tried to isolate her motives, the more aware I became that I had stopped hurting over Vance and the more I felt a sinister glee to see through her motives.

I perked up and focused on her. "I'm good. I'm just worried about the end of the term. Lots to plan during break. I've got a puzzle of my own to deal with there, but it will keep. What have you got for me?" I drank deeply from the cup while she pulled up the information. The liquid was warm to begin with and began to burn before I stopped. Pain, it turns out, was also a powerful focusing tool.

She handed me the pad and went back to the kitchen while I studied it. I watched her over the top of the pad as she left. She wasn't heading for anything. She just wanted to be away from me while I worked.

The pad was heavy with data this time. Instead of a one-floor plan, there were three. A total of ten floors to the building in question with a target room listed on the third floor above ground with two more below a basement and sub-basement.

The second-floor plan showed retrofitting and changes to the first layout. The third showed conjectured changes since the second plan. The first challenge was in determining what changes were more likely than not.

The next set of information was about entry points and exits. The facility was Union, something important as it showed signs of internal defense from the Union military as well as technology purchased from Klemtite and Chrysalis.

For a moment, it seemed like DSS had no presence in the building, but then I saw the internal human-manned monitoring station. The best of all worlds, or at least that was the projection of force at work.

The final set of information addressed personnel and staff movements—guard shifts and patterns of projected movement. The duty roster and employee access logs were sparse. Essential personnel only.

There was nothing in the way of utility and service lines. I saw why this was as well. Everything was internal and self-contained. Even the water waste was collected and manually taken out and in. It wasn't efficient, but it sure as hell was secure.

I put down the pad and saw Evelyn lurking through the island window. "I've got what I need to start. Anything specific you need to tell me about the goal?"

As she came back into the living area, I noticed that her bedroom door was wide open. She caught my gaze then walked over to the door and secured it. She gave me a quick smile, "Now now, young man, a woman's inner chamber is not for your eyes."

She affected the adult scolding a child tone as a distraction. I saw two things in the room that I couldn't forget. The first was a stock certificate related to Chronos Edu Inc., the same place that secured my school funding. Possibly a coincidence, but a peculiar one. The other was a photo of Evelyn and an older man. The pose suggested a familiarity, but formally so. Perhaps it was distant relative or a professional contact. The thing that was most shocking was that the man in the photo was Canton's father.

She sat in the wingback chair and picked up the pad, then she flipped through the data screens until she saw something she needed to comment on. "This here." She showed me the slide. "That box is the target, which you knew. What you didn't know is that it can't be moved without special tools."

"Will we have access to those tools?"

She laughed. "Of course. Wouldn't be much of a heist if we couldn't take the loot out. All you need to figure out is how to find a window of time to get the box out. The wider the better, obviously."

I drank the rest of my beverage. "I'll get to work. When I have an answer, I will message you."

She patted me on the knee. "I wait patiently, but not very. I'm counting on you to really dazzle me with your brilliance this time. Now let yourself out. I have other things to attend to."

I WORKED on the problem through the evening and late into the night. It was a formidable task in scope and structure. The number of floors below and above the target meant covering a lot of ground on both an approach and an exit.

The internal, self-contained nature of the utilities eliminated cutting off vital services and there would be no sneaking in as faux maintenance staff. Everything was maintained by a dedicated, around-the-clock set of technicians that lived inside the complex. The expense to maintain the facility must have been immense, but you get what you pay for.

The guard patrols were the final hurdle. Their paths through the facility didn't give enough time to make any pathway through feasible. Moving through one, even two floors without running into a patrol was conceivable, but not three or more, which meant a pathway into the facility was possible, but exiting would be more difficult. Moving the box made taking the same route back out a whole new challenge.

Of course, the routing was a lost cause because there were no useful entrances. The roof had an access portal and a landing pad for aerial transports. It also had a complete guard station and a single elevator that linked further into the complex. The front door had two checkpoint areas with an external bunker that had to be crossed before entering the building itself. Neither the basement nor the sub-basement had any external outlet. They were accessible only through an elevator system. Only a few floors had stairs that linked them with most of the complex being connected by elevators that crossed only two or three stories.

Each time I hit a seemingly impossible section, I turned my attention to another aspect of the problem. I was trying to figure out one element and then use what I knew would work to connect the next. It took me three passes through the basic elements of infiltrate, secure, exfiltrate before I came up with even one path that could avoid guards, and it only worked if we started inside the building at particular points.

I worked it down to key phases and difficulties.

The first was security technology. In previous jobs, we were able to overcome the devices with an array of exploits and knowing the placement of each system. Those setups were straightforward: determine a pathway to the target and then plan to eliminate each obstacle along the way. The changing nature of the obstacles in the way and not knowing exactly which company was supplying potentially overlapping systems meant more time at each obstacle to defeat and move past.

The second problem was guards. The patrols were well-thought-out and the number of guards for the facility was in excess of what would be needed for any other facility of size. Still, they did patrol and didn't simply post man-to-man zones. Briefly, I wondered if this was to make it seem possible while remaining undoable. It was far more likely to be a practical matter of keeping the guards alert. You also couldn't bribe or disable a single guard to breach an area. They traveled in packs of three, which would make them the equal of any infiltration group. A solo agent wouldn't have time to disable enough of the technology to proceed.

Time was the next problem. Any route in would need to disable enough systems to mask the route out without running into maintenance staff or guards.

I considered three different tiers of success. Getting out clean, getting out but being noticed, and getting the box out but losing everyone on the way.

I faded into a stressful sleep as I considered this last set of parameters. What level of sacrifice was I willing to suggest? What level could I even imagine?

I STRUGGLED through classes the next day. The lack of sleep from the past few days was taking its toll. Between thinking about the Union puzzle and considering what to do about the Vance situation, I hadn't slept a full night in over a week. Coupled with that was my severe disinterest in class. Nothing that they were teaching was applicable in the worlds I had been moving in. It was just facts and data, which I could look up or memorize. Theory was lacking and practical application even less common.

Still, maintenance was important. I managed through the day and walked to the track afterward. It was a place that I could keep myself alert while I thought through issues. It was also where Vance's influence and life philosophy seemed strongest.

I passed by the athletic building and onto the track area proper, when I saw Manson and Gil. They were hovering around the far side of the track, looking grim. They waved me over, and I nodded. It was a strong departure from the way they greeted me during my first night at Quintell—a testament to Vance's ability to create allies and weave people together. His sociability was something I'd always lacked, and now I found myself missing it.

"What are we going to do, Alphonse?" Manson asked

"We can't do nothing." Gil scoffed.

I waved my arms in exhaustion and leaned down to start my stretches. "I'm here to exercise."

Manson dropped down and followed my technique. "We need to talk about Vance. I know he's gone, but we can do something. Can't we?"

"Do something about what?" I asked. "Vance is gone."

Gil didn't bother stretching. Instead, he began to pace around the two of us. "He's talking about Canton. I'll say it. Canton needs to go down."

I stood up and walked to the nearby wall of the athletic club for the next set of stretches. "I've been thinking about that," I said. It was tough to admit, but they sounded like they were on the verge of something rash. Knowing those two, I expected something crude and simple, like a straightforward brawl in the bathroom. I needed to work with them, or I would lose any opportunity at Canton myself.

Manson again copied my actions. "We're thinking we can make his life hell. Just a little. Show him what it's like."

Gil bounced up and down, waiting for us to get moving. "I just wanna deck him and be done with it."

I sighed. "That means you're gone and Canton looks like a proper student menaced. You can't hurt him publicly like that."

We started a lap around the track. The motion helped me think. It was admittedly nice to have them with me.

Manson gasped and wheezed even on the warm-up lap. Gil, of course, had boundless energy.

He jogged in front of me a few paces and turned around the way Vance would have. "We should poison him," he said, casually.

I stopped running and feigned a shoe adjustment, and Manson was happy to stop and catch his breath. I spoke in a quiet tone. "What do you mean, *poison?*"

Gil took part of the hint and lowered his voice for parts of the statement. "Not like, to death or really badly. Just something that will hurt and make him look like a chump. Like when I took that dare and ate all those chilis. I didn't die, but I kinda felt like I might."

I considered the possibility. "Something like food poisoning. Something that would not be traced and would give him problems."

Gil and Manson both nodded. "Yeah, especially if he puked in class or couldn't get excused and ruined some pants. That would be great."

Public humiliation didn't have the same effect or permanence as expulsion, but it might do for the short-term. Still, I wondered if such a thing was beneath me. I stood up and started into my next lap. "Let me think about it. I'll let you know what I come up with."

I started running and they followed. We did a few laps before Manson had to take a breather. Overall, it was good exercise.

I RETURNED to my room and got back to work on the problem. Manson and Gil had one thing right—some low-grade food poisoning could be a good way to disrupt people without being suspicious. I checked some information on the network and discovered productivity in the workplace dropped by thirty percent when employees were ill. Even better, response times to critical tasks fell as much as forty-five percent.

Bouts of food-borne illness could last seventy-two hours with extreme symptoms not being noticed upwards of sixteen hours after exposure. If enough employees were given different tainted meals within a day of a planned job, they would be sluggish and ill-prepared to deal with emergencies. Being a Union complex, a place where highly-trained and elite workers operated, they wouldn't fail to report to work for minor problems.

By the time they realized the problems were more than minor, the whole facility would be in a sad state.

It was a risky plan, as the behaviors of each individual would vary widely. It could also cause delays in patrols, which would make avoiding guards even harder. If there was a way to affect different groups of employees with different types of illness, that would give the best tactical advantage.

Working a series of illnesses targeted at the security monitors, maintenance staff, and guards provided far wider gaps in patrol times and repairs of crucial systems. It also bogged down the internal air and water filtration systems. As the problems became obvious, they would attempt to reinforce key areas and suspect breaches at the doors. This would make exfiltration harder.

I concluded that three distinct food-borne illnesses would create manageable havoc. This gave me options in moving other key pieces of the complex problem, but it didn't provide a full solution. I retreated to sleep excited to be making progress but worried that I had so far yet to go.

THE NEXT DAY swept by less slowly since I'd had some rest. Still, the problem was not solved, and the Canton issue also needed something definitive. I hoped to gain some space to concentrate more fully on the puzzle, so I decided to visit Mr. Kurns and glean something about Canton's financial situation. Maybe he could be exposed without taking down Mr. Kurns's whole system.

I hurried from my final class in the history building to the maintenance building in hopes of catching Mr. Kurns before he left for the day. His schedule was idiosyncratic, either as part of his extracurricular affairs or the pressures of working an on-call job.

Fortunately, he was in his office. I knocked on the door when I saw him sitting at his desk. He waved to me and hit a button, then the door released and I entered. The door shut behind me. "You might want to catch the blinds."

I did as suggested, pulling the blinds down over the office window and door.

Mr. Kurns put up a hand in warning and pointed to a seat. "I know why you're here. Sit down and listen before you get in trouble."

I took a seat. His tone was conciliatory, not angry. Whatever he was referring to had nothing to do with my own extracurricular pursuits.

He stitched his hands together beneath his salt and pepper beard. "It's troubling what happened to Vance. Nothing to do about it. He was in over his head and dealing with people that were sloppy. I told him it was bad business, but he said he could work it out."

I smiled. "You could remove his arms and legs and Vance would still say he had things under control." I bit my lip and balled up a fist. "It was his best and most frustrating quality."

Mr. Kurns laughed. "Sounds like you knew him well. So, do you have anything specific for me?"

I considered the offer. Though the scope of the tone was broad, I went for the direct approach. "I need to know what kind of deals you have with Canton. How much he's been allotted and where he squanders it. I know that his father's company provides his school support, but I assume he has you double-dipping on that."

Mr. Kurns shrugged and pulled up a file on his data pad. "Right to it, then, no cat and mouse about what each of us knows. I appreciate that. Canton spends money like he has an endless supply. Mind you, with the value of his father's company, that isn't too far from the truth. His father tries to cut him off from time to time, but Canton is resourceful."

"No. He's abusive. There's a difference."

Mr. Kurns flipped to a spreadsheet on the pad. "True enough." He pointed to a section of highlighted lines on the spreadsheet. "See here? These deductions happened after his last cut off. He failed a bio exam, so his father stopped the transfers. He had me lift twice as much for what he called *incentive and compensation*."

I saw another set of higher-end numbers. "What about these? Those seem to be even higher."

Mr. Kurns shook his head. "That's why you don't over-reward and under-punish. Soon as he passed the next exam, highest grade in the class thanks to Vance's provided answers, his dad upped his weekly by more than he took away."

"What would happen, do you think, if Canton failed a test bad enough to fail the term?"

Mr. Kurns suppressed a glimmer in his eyes. "If some miracle arranged that, he'd head home for the break with no cash flow and an angry father. It might not stick, but it would be a helluva a slap to his shit-muncher ego."

I had a thought about the shell game that Mr. Kurns ran with maintenance and supplies. "How do you deal with heavy shifts in cash flow between your two activities?"

He turned off the pad and stood up before walking to a rack of parts on the far side of the small office. "In the lean times, you make do. In the heavy times, you stock up on a few things. I've been doing this a long time and I know how to chart the winds, as it were."

"And people that don't have your experience?"

Mr. Kurns chuckled. "They start with putting in more effort to compensate for the right materials, and as it gets worse, they start blaming the supply chain. Eventually, they curse the tools that work for not being magical. They rarely notice they were the weak component in the system."

"Thank you, Mr. Kurns. For the information, and the kind words about Vance. Please, go ahead and keep my weekly allowance."

He shook his head and walked me to the door. "I appreciate the offer, Alphonse, but you keep what is yours and I'll keep what's mine. This conversation didn't happen." He gave me a broad wink and opened the door. "I'll see what I can do about that hallway door," he said as a cover.

"It has been bothering me since I arrived."

I HEADED BACK to my room and began working on the next step for the Canton plan. I needed to get him a message that I could help him with his bio final. That would set him up for the failure I had in mind.

As for the Evelyn puzzle, Mr. Kurns had given me some insight into the maintenance world. Engineers thought they were smarter than the problems they encountered. They would be more prone to try and fix a problem with bad resources than admit they couldn't.

If the supply of parts for the complex dried up, they would continue to operate and do work around that would lead to cascading failures. Union regulations were publicly accessible, so I checked through them. All essential systems were required to have redundancies and parts on hand. But they only needed to have one extra of anything. Even a cautious engineer would only have two.

Tampering with the supply chain would be difficult. Either replacing the shipments headed for the facility with broken parts that the engineers would work around or freezing their budgets to order just long enough to have them bottom out of the reserves seemed like the best choices. It would be difficult to do both without it being suspicious. Still, I had another wedge to open up the facility. The plan was becoming clear, bit by bit.

17

THE NEXT DAY, I was removed from classes early. My previous deception about the clinic appointment needed a second phase. The doctor I had scheduled an impossible meeting with to check up on Whiles had now officially started office hours. With my general lack of sleep and stress, it seemed like it would provide me with a good baseline for creating smoke screens in the future.

I hadn't been to many doctors in my life. I knew what to avoid and practiced careful handwashing and general cleanliness. Disease was about happenstance and nobody was immune forever, but I had expressed proper caution in the past, which had kept me safe enough.

I proceeded to the gate and was stopped by Proctor Maevik with her usual confused wave/salute greeting.

"Alphonse? You're with me, no bus for a middle of day journey."

I should have known that. Clearly, the sleep deprivation was wearing on me more than I was able to express. "Good to see you, Proctor Maevik."

She frowned. "What did I tell you about using my last name? Cams will do. It really is alright. I'm staff, you don't have to be formal with me like faculty."

She walked with me back from the gate to the maintenance shed and the transport already set to go. I didn't see Mr. Kurns.

"I was taught to use the name appropriate to the situation, nicknames and first names being for peers. You still hold a position of authority. I would hate to negate that."

She sighed and got in the transport. "I don't know if I should be flattered that you think being a glorified truant officer has authority or mad that you're using it as an excuse. Either way, we have to be at the clinic soon."

Maevik navigated the route there as quickly as she navigated her way through crowds. Despite the traffic, we arrived early. And since it was a clinic office, even somewhat late is still early. The Union might have the transports running on time, but medicine would always be a field that takes a lot of time and never runs true to schedule.

The admitting staff took my name and confirmed the doctor's name. "Scheduled for 1:20? Well, it's 1:10 now, so we'll get to you as soon as the doctor is available. Take a seat"—they checked the paperwork—"Alphonse."

I sat down and Maevik took up a position beside me. The waiting room was, of course, packed. We took the last two seats near the general clinic door. I was quiet, studying the faces of the other patients waiting. I idly diagnosed them based on their reactions and external symptoms. Or tried. It didn't take long before I realized I couldn't tell who was a patient and who was a supporter. Illness has a fear effect that masks true intentions. People simply don't know how to act like themselves when faced with fear and apprehension. Too much instinct to maintain individuality for the most part.

A technician emerged from the clinic and checked a pad and then called out a name and a time stamp. "Broadkle? 12:40?"

Maevik sighed and I met her gaze. They were three people behind. The technician also caught her sigh and looked at us. There was a flash of recognition. "Captain Maevik? Good to see you. Are you here for an adjustment? Oh my, your wig is looking excellent. I knew that they would get you a proper fit."

Maevik concealed a mixture of rage and embarrassment. "Alphonse, I'll be at the transport. Lydia, everything's fine." She pushed through the door and exited in a hurry.

Lydia, the technician, looked horrified. She had broken protocol and made a terrible faux pas in drawing attention to Maevik in an open space. Not that anyone else in the space was paying attention. She fixed me with a look and then greeted Mr. Broadkle, then she escorted him down the hall and was gone for several minutes.

I returned to my deliberations on the actions of the waiting room people, but also considered what I had learned about Maevik. Lydia returned and sat beside me. "Are you a friend or relative of Camille?"

"No, I'm a student at Quintell Academy. Proctor Maevik is my escort for the clinic appointment."

She looked chagrined. "I'm so sorry about before. I hadn't seen her almost a year. We… knew each other before. Let her know I apologize and will accept any formal complaint she may want to file." She stood up. "I have to get back to work."

It was over an hour before I was finally called in. Predictably, my appointment took only the twenty allotted minutes as I explained my situation and he performed routine tests. My lack of questions and general ability to follow instruction made everything go smoothly.

Afterward, I returned to the transport to find Maevik standing outside at attention. She was visibly shaken by the experience, her usual open and jovial nature missing. She stood at attention with a cold, nearly robotic posture. I approached the transport and stopped before getting in. She watched me intently, not moving.

"The technician, Lydia, wanted me to pass along an apology. I would also like to apologize, Cams."

She shot me a cold look then opened the door. I also entered the transport.

"Don't give me that out of sympathy, Mr. M . . . Alphonse." She struggled to land on a name for me. In the end, she sighed. The transport remained off and unmoving.

"I didn't understand before how important the dynamic of authority and peer was to you," I explained. "In there, Lydia exposed several secrets you don't want known. I'm sorry that you had to go through that. But I will call you by the name you request, because that is respect. A formal title doesn't define who you are, but how people should see you. An offered name says something about who you want to be. I see that now."

She sighed and started the transport. "Apology accepted. Let's get back to campus, Alphonse."

As we moved out of the clinic area and onto the road, I had an idea. "We're already out and it isn't unreasonable for a student to request a comfort stop after a clinic visit, is it?"

She nodded. "Do you need to go somewhere? You don't seem like the clinic bothered you."

"No. I'm fine . . . it's for you. I would like to buy you a cake and coffee."

She laughed a dry chuckle. "I appreciate the offer. I'll even take you up on it." She turned toward the downtown area. Within minutes, we'd arrived at a hole-in-the-wall café. "This is my favorite," she commented.

We exited the transport and put in an order, then sat down.

"Do you want to know the whole story?"

I considered what I already knew and what I didn't, then decided it would be prudent not to blurt what I knew. "Anything you want to tell. I don't need all of your secrets."

She smiled, more herself in that moment. The coffee and

cakes arrived. She was even a bit animated in accepting them. "This café is run by something of an expat. A former soldier living on a Union world. He's an interesting guy. I was Union military myself. Stationed out in the rim worlds near the Deadlands."

I nodded and enjoyed the coffee. It had a bit of spice to it.

"I was part of a search and recovery team," she said. "Second in the chain under a tough nut of a commander, Jack Welder. He pushed us beyond what we thought we could do, which is good for a commanding officer. He also backed us when things went wrong and we lost people." She sipped her coffee and enjoyed some cake. "Search and recovery is a difficult job. We were trained to extricate assets, usually black boxes and prototypes, occasionally pilots and VIPs, from extreme conditions—crashes on hostile worlds, accessing derelicts that had lost life support. Anything could go wrong, and we could lose our target or members of the squad." She rubbed her right arm and I heard her shuffling her feet. "We were good at what we did. Even the missions that went poorly were rarely a complete disaster."

I couldn't hold my tongue any longer and interjected, "You lost the arm and both legs below the knee. From what Lydia implied, you also had some skull rebuilt that left you unable to grow your own hair. It looks natural, by the way."

She fought for a moment to scowl or smile, settling on a pained grin. "I've noticed you do a good job of reading people. Surprised it took you this long to say anything."

I put down my coffee. "I'm learning. To not upset people.

You were reserved about your personal history. I didn't want to take from you, Cams. The salute/wave you do. That is a brain issue, right? A programming mistake?"

Now she was impressed. "Yes. Whenever I want to greet someone, it goes to muscle memory and that memory spent fifteen years saluting, so it fights to do both. Both gestures access the same storage in the brain, and it comes out wrong."

"The same with your feet then, the shuffling is you fighting to be still and to be ready at the same time?"

She frowned and took a heavy sigh. "No. That one is a remnant of their last action as they jerked to get me away from the hull breach that tore me apart. No matter what I do, somewhere in my mind, they're always in motion."

I had nothing to say to that. The losses I had faced in life didn't mean anything. I didn't care enough to mourn my parents, and though I missed Vance, it was nothing in comparison.

She drained the rest of her coffee and moved around the remaining crumbs of her cake. "Alphonse. Thanks for this. It was helpful. When you close yourself off but leave a way for people to get under your skin, it just leads to disaster, you know?"

I didn't know. But I had a flash of inspiration.

IT TOOK a few hours of digging on the network, but my hunch paid off. Maevik's situation gave me the idea and I had to run down the details to confirm it was possible. I sent Evelyn a message that night then headed over, hoping she would be ready for me.

As I approached the Cascade Gardens, I saw that she was waiting for me by the stoop, cigarette in hand. I gave her a cheerful wave, a bit too excited. I tried to calm down as I crossed the park.

"We'll talk inside," she said as she snuffed out the cigarette.

As usual, I gathered the butt as she opened the door.

Once we were inside the apartment, she sat in the wing-back chair. "Alright, tell me what you have that's worth interrupting me at this hour."

I noticed that she hadn't removed her coat at the door as she usually did. She also had a bit of the scent of wine on her. "You'll want to get your data pad and take notes. It isn't a simple solution," I explained.

She perked up at that. "Go make us some tea in the kitchen."

It was an odd request. I had never been further into her apartment than the sofa I was sitting on. I did as instructed and walked into the kitchen. The kettle and cups were in plain sight, so I did the preparation. I could hear her entering and then exiting and resealing her bedroom.

I took the tea back to the living area and sat in my usual spot. She was ready with her data pad.

"There are three major components to the plan," I said.

She fixed me with her half smile. "Oh, nothing more elegant and one trick beats all?"

Her words expressed mockery, but her tone was one of admiration. "The three steps cover the major issues of entrance, guard patrols, and security bypass needed to get in and out cleanly."

She nodded. "Drink your tea and walk me through it slowly."

I poured myself a cup and continued on. "The most important part is the infiltration route. Nothing was working when I tried to plot a path through any of the known entrances. The front door was an immediate problem; we wouldn't even get through the outer bunker into the complex proper. The roof access only got us to the sixth floor. Service entrances ended with us being picked off and only hitting the fourth floor at best."

She nodded and traced her finger over her pad, following my logic.

"I was puzzled by part of the construction of the basement into the sub-basement. These spaces are irregular in shape to the floors above. That meant they were built at a different time than the rest of the complex, apparently as part of a shelter years ago. A disused sewer line once connected to them but was walled off when the new complex was built."

She lit up at that.

"I sent you an updated schematic with the sewer line," I said.

She accessed the plan and her smile grew. "Well well."

"It would take weeks to dig through the rock," I continued. "It's only fifty feet, but any drilling will arouse suspicion except for an hour between three and four when the maintenance team runs a check on their seismograph. While the system is calibrating, they won't register any of the vibrations. Guards also check the entrances to the sewer line before and after the calibration. A driller would need to be down there for as much as ten hours for each hour of drilling to avoid detection."

She made some notes. "And the other two steps of your solution?"

"To create as many windows of opportunity to defeat the security inside, you would need to starve out the supplies of the maintenance teams. This means cutting payment flow high enough up the chain that it started interfering with compensation for the workers and the suppliers. This will upset the maintenance teams and force work with inadequate supplies and parts."

Again, Evelyn beamed as she wrote down information. "So that anything that went down when someone accessed the box, they wouldn't know if it was intruders or typical problems. Interesting."

I gave a slight nod. "The third part is to find the catering companies bringing food into the complex. Introducing some contaminated ingredients into the food will infect most of the workers with low-level illnesses a day after the sabotage. This will limit overall response times and cause confusion during the aftermath. The complex would be upset at the catering company but won't be able to prove anything connected to a third party."

Evelyn looked through the information she had written. "Very good, Alphonse. I almost thought you were going to be stumped by this one. Color me impressed."

I sighed. The relief from the days of work in coming up with such a difficult series of solutions had weighed on me even more than I thought. "So that was the answer?" I asked.

Evelyn looked at the pad and back at me. "Of course. Yes, can't slide anything past you. Now I've got to get back to some other matters. Return to your room and I'll contact you again soon."

I headed to the door, expecting her to follow, but she was still busy with the pad. So I let myself out.

18

I SPENT the next three days putting my plan for Canton in place. The first part was going to be the most difficult, so I saw to it quickly.

Manson and Gil had been meeting me at the track after classes most afternoons. It was good exercise, which we needed, but it was also a kind of informal and unspoken "remember Vance" group.

I wasn't surprised to hear Gil talking in his excited, unrestrained clip while Manson interjected surly warnings in between. The subject of their banter: Canton's imminent poisoning.

"Botulism," Gil stated. "It's so easy. We can get some from all sorts of places. They use it for like, medical things. It will look like he's just into that stuff."

"Not so loud, idiot," Manson warned him.

They came around the corner, where I was already done with my stretches and prepped to run. "Botulism toxin also can cause death. So, no."

Gil shrugged. "How am I supposed to know what's deadly and what's just bad?"

Manson sighed and tugged on his shoes. "We learned in chem class. Pay attention, man."

Gil looked shocked. "I only remember the useful stuff. How to make fuel and smells and explosion. Y'know? Useful."

I jogged in place, impatient to get started. "We shouldn't poison him with anything."

Gil bounced around Manson and got up close to me. "What you mean? Do nothing?"

Manson stood up and did a few half-hearted stretches. "He didn't say do nothing, just no poisoning."

Gil bounced back to get in Manson's space. "That's nothing, isn't it?"

Manson stepped past the exuberant youth and started into a lap. "It's different, but it sounds dumb. We gotta do something, Alphonse."

I ran along with him and Gil quickly caught up and got in front of us. "There are other ways to get to Canton. Look, if he gets ill, that can be an excuse he will use to explain failing his classes."

Manson struggled to speak through his usual wheezing. "Oh yeah. We want him to fail. Get him kicked out or held back. Man, that's embarrassing."

Gil did a circle around us in joy. "Can you imagine his

face? That would be crucial. How you going to make that happen?"

"I'm working on it. I just need you two to calm down and stop loudly discussing poisoning. There will be a part for you to play. Just give me some more time."

They exchanged a glance. "Okay, Alphonse. We trust you. Do Vance proud."

Gil chimed in with the last word. "Just make sure we're there to see it."

We finished our run and I headed back to my room to shower and change. As I closed my door, I saw that I'd received a message from Evelyn. She wanted me to meet up with her at Winston's apartment.

I ARRIVED and Evelyn was already inside when I knocked. "I take it this is a job call?" I asked as she opened the door.

She was dismissive and just busied herself, tidying bits of Winston's usual mess and saying nothing. Evelyn had never been very talkative, but today was different. Something about her breathing and the lack of eye contact made me wonder if she had something on her mind.

Before I could ask, there was another knock at the door, and Evelyn waved me to answer it. I did, revealing Remi on the other side. He quickly slipped in and cleared his throat. "No Winston?" he said without looking.

"I just arrived. I figured he was out doing an errand," I remarked.

Evelyn put down a discolored throw pillow. "Yes. Winston will be out for a few weeks. He's doing some personal things and I'm looking after his place." She slapped the pillow a few times and watched a spray of dust come out. "Somebody clearly needs to."

Remi sidestepped the dust cloud and stood along the wall near the door. "Fine. What are we dealing with today?"

Evelyn stopped pretending to cough in the dust cloud she had created and picked up a data pad. "You two are going on a quick smash and grab at a personnel staffing office."

Remi nodded. "No prep work, just in and out?"

Evelyn laughed. "I may have overstated the smashing part. You'll be making a return to your Klemtite Essentials silent working duo personas. The building is uptown, past the financial center but well east of the Union dispatch station. I don't like to put you too close to previous areas."

Remi remained expressionless. I was annoyed that nothing sounded exciting or challenging. Routine sounded like something that didn't need or interest me. I would rather spend time working on the Canton plan.

She seemed to sense our disinterest. "Before you two professionals get all sullen on me, there is a catch." She projected a picture above her pad. "This is the new Chrysalis door we've been hearing about. The building just installed them. Just like the previous models, they require special isotope keys to open. As an improvement, they also require

that key to synchronize with ELF frequencies within designated key holders."

Remi frowned. "How are we supposed to get through
that?"

Evelyn laughed. "False I.D.'s have already been made.
You are Klemtite's best security officers, trying to show that
Chrysalis is wrong to home in on their biometrics market
share. At least, that's why you're in the building."

I filled in the blank. "So, if we *do* get caught, we're just
two workers. No harm. Except that we may have to lose the
identities."

She nodded.

Remi remained unconvinced. "How is the kid supposed to
pass himself off as a security professional?"

"Oh, that's the best part, Remi. He's your trainee. And if
anyone can see a flaw in the design, it will be Alphonse."

REMI PULLED the Klemtite Essentials van up to the service
entrance and we got out. The building was a solid tower, one
of several in the area. Unlike the financial district buildings,
which often had a lot of glass and odd external architecture to
show off the wealth of the companies inhabiting them, this
was rather plain.

I fetched the usual gear bag from the back and Remi
strapped on his tool harness. We entered the lobby and met
the security inside. There were two guards at the desk, along

with a business representative from Chrysalis Motivations. He had all the earmarks of a middle manager: the fidgety hand and slicked back hair, the eyes trying to look for an angle but just moving too much. He greeted us as we entered.

"Welcome to our little test, gentleman and . . . assistant."

His glance at me confused, as if he was expecting two people, but not the two he was seeing. For a moment, I was concerned that we were going to get caught before we got started.

He kept going after his delay. "You are here to try and breach the offices on the fourteenth floor. These belong to a staffing company that has recently acquired some high-end Union service contracts and needs to prove they have the security to defend their information."

He paused again and reached out to shake our hands, first reaching for me and making a show of reaching down for my hand despite the fact that I was, at best, four inches shorter than him. Then he shook hands with Remi, and I saw recognition. There was more going on in the moment than was being spoken.

"Now. Your job here is also to do your best for Klemtite Essentials. It goes without saying that Chrysalis Motivations is counting on you failing to show the superiority of their new product."

He concluded his boisterous introduction by turning around and leading us to the elevator. We stopped outside and he punched a button to call the car. "We'll be down here waiting." He gestured to the two guards. "We won't be monitoring the floor with cameras. Klemtite was adamant that no record-ings or monitoring of your intrusion devices could be made."

The car arrived and we got in.

Before the doors shut, the manager made a final state-ment. "We'll be up quickly to let you out when you fail. You can try any trick you want. Use everything you have hiding up your sleeves, but Chrysalis Motivations knows that our tech is unbeatable."

The doors closed and the elevator ascended. I looked to Remi. "Do you think they actually won't record us?"

He considered for a moment. "Corporations have some heft to protect their tech. It's possible. I say always act like you're being watched. It's the only real way to go."

The elevator stopped and we exited into an antechamber. In front of us was the Exquisite Staffing and Personnel office. The stylization on the first letter of each word, in combina-tion with the color, gave me the impression they wanted to convey the acronym ESP for the company. It was smart branding. It was easier to say and remember and it allowed them to imply they had a "sixth sense" about staffing needs. I imagined they must have advertisements with those exact words in them.

The front doors were meant to be opened during business hours and led only to an outer office. Remi worked the clicker and had the door open before I had finished all of my initial observations. We entered the outer office and saw that we had a choice of two impressive versions of Chrysalis Motivation's signature door.

The one on the left had a keypad next to an almost archaic-sized keyhole. The algorithm controlled when the door could be opened, and the keyhole was the entrance to the isotope lock.

The one on the right had only a flat black panel in the middle of the door with two small circular indentations about a hand's width apart.

The doors were recessed down hallways about eight feet. Remi gestured to the ceiling, and I saw that recessed bulkheads waited to slide down and trap us if we failed to access the doors. My research on Chrysalis suggested this was the way things worked, but it was interesting to see confirmation of the deep network theories.

I shrugged and pointed left and then right.

Remi nodded and pointed to the door on the right first. He took the gear bag from me and winked as he headed to the left door.

I took up position at the panel on the right door while Remi stood at the panel on the left. He pulled out a few tools from the bag. Nonsense tools, from the looks of it. Nothing he produced would disrupt the algorithm or let him pick the isotope lock. At best, they might let him cut through the door in a few days, assuming nothing broke or shorted on him.

He saw me watching him and gave me a stern look, then he gave me the signal for eyes forward and pointed at my door. A moment later, he sparked up a cutting torch and the bulkhead on his side slammed shut.

At a loss for how to proceed, I worked my way through

the conversation with the manager in the lobby below. He seemed to be telling Remi something. For that brief moment, they also acted like they had seen each other before, or at least knew a call sign to recognize each other. His parting words were incongruous with the rest of his language. I checked my own sleeve.

There was a small metal strip there. I pulled it out and found that it opened. Inside was a small patch meant to be attached to the wrist, so I pressed it on and then placed my thumb and pinky on the indentations on the panel. The door slid open. I walked by and it slid into place behind me.

Now in the inner office, but devoid of any tools, I started hunting around for the ID card. There were several desks, all empty, and a row of filing cabinets against the wall. I inspected the filing cabinets and found that each of them had a panel similar to the one on the door. Again, I pressed my thumb and pinky into the indentations, and one after another, the cabinets opened. I found the target ID, put it in my jump-suit, and ran back to the hallway. Another touch took me back through the prototype door and into the outer office. I made it to the sealed bulkhead that was trapping Remi in time for the security guards and manager to emerge from the elevator.

The guards were smiling, but the manager was practically giddy. I hadn't removed the device from my wrist, so I put my hand deep in my pocket and did my best to look caught and upset.

They came into the outer office and were audibly laugh-ing. The manager pointed to me. "I wish we had been able to record you. The look on your face when that bulkhead came down and separated you. Oh boy. I'm surprised you didn't wet yourself." When I didn't respond, he said, "Oh, don't be like that. Fine, just keep your hands in your pockets and touch nothing while we get your dad out."

The other guards were working on punching in the code and keying open the door. "Stand back, kid. No reason for you to get exposed to this." The other guard opened a metal box on his belt and pulled out a large key. He fitted it into the lock and turned, and the bulkhead slid away.

Beyond it, Remi was doing his best to look scared and surprised. He was also trying to shove tools into the gear bag and cover what he had been using at the same time.

"Don't bother," said one guard. "Nothing you have there worked. Who cares if we see it?"

"I take my work seriously," Remi said in an unaffected tone. "I'm not letting you take our secrets."

The guards laughed again. "The only secret here is you're going to be out of a job when your whole company goes down. Chrysalis has the edge now."

Remi finished shoving everything in the gear bag and came into the outer office. "C'mon kid, we've been humiliated enough tonight."

The manager gave a dismissive wave but then followed us into the elevator. He called back to the guards, "You finish resetting here, I'll escort them out."

We boarded the elevator, and the doors closed.

Remi stood quietly in the corner and I kept my hands

jammed into the pockets of my jumpsuit. After a few floors, the manager spoke up. "No recording devices in here. You did great."

Remi nodded. "Everything as planned."

The manager looked to me. "Good idea using the kid. Tossed all their suspicion. Hey, kid, don't ever let anyone know you have that thing. Destroy it as soon as you're out of here. We're talking major corporate espionage charge."

We reached the lobby. As we walked out, the manger put on a show for any prying eyes. "Your dad here is probably getting the ol' pink slip tomorrow. Better hold on to your savings. Goodbye and thanks for playing."

We stored our gear back in the transport and took off.

When we were a few blocks out, Remi started talking. "Good work catching onto the plan. Evelyn wasn't sure you had the acting to pull it off, so we kept you in the dark, but I knew you would figure it out. If you're wondering, the manager will play the stock on Chrysalis and invest in Klemtite before he defects over there. They'll take a huge hit when it gets out how easy their prototype is to defeat, but for now, they will look strong."

I considered the small patch on my wrist and the ramifications of having it. I had no intention of destroying it, no matter the risk. I needed to know what it was before I made any decision.

Remi's point about the manager, though—that struck a chord. People always did their worst when they thought they had won. For my Canton plan to work, I had to make him feel like he was in charge. I would have to gain his confidence and then give him the wrong answers as an apology. He would never doubt what I sold to him.

DESPITE THE WEIGHT of the major puzzle being lifted and my plan for Canton well underway, I found it difficult to sleep. I had a nagging ache in my thoughts about how things were going. The initial thrill I had felt overcoming the challenges in a heist had faded. The puzzles had occupied me for a time, but now I was out of things to do.

The loss of Vance and the need to see Canton pay for his actions ran deep, but it wasn't enough. I struggled to put the pieces of my drive together.

As I tossed in bed, I went back to the question Mr. Black had asked me about my future. I'd had more time to consider the answer and still I had nothing satisfying. My talks with Vance and Remi had made it clear that shaping a future was more important than choosing one.

I got on the network and patched a message through Vance's empty room to Evelyn. I wanted a distraction and hoped she would have something to give me.

Do you have anything? I'm sure you heard about the recent job. Went smoothly. Looking for something more challenging. – A

I stared at the screen for some time, going back and forth

between willing a response out of the cosmos and trying to relax so I could sleep.

Finally, a message came through.

Open communication? You know better than that. Nothing going on for now. Bigger gears in motion. Everything will come together. Relax and save energy. You will need it for the future. – E

I turned off the pad and stared at the dark ceiling. Everything was going too well and not well enough. I should have been content but wasn't. I resigned myself to not knowing, for now. Eventually, sleep came.

19

THE NEXT SEVERAL weeks were busy but unfulfilling. Per the plan, I began showing off in biology and chemistry classes.

These were the classes I shared with Canton. I was quick to comment about how simple and obvious all of the answers were. I even responded to a few questions before they were fully asked to give the impression that I knew something beyond the in-class information.

My days continued this way for a time. Meanwhile, my nights were filled with planning as I, along with Evelyn and Remi, continued executing small and profitable jobs.

AFTER NEARLY A WEEK, Evelyn had cleaned up a lot of

Winston's place. The dirt was gone, and the apartment no longer carried a heavy lived-in odor.

"You are infiltrating an industrial fabrication complex," explained Evelyn, shortly after Remi and I had taken our seats. "You'll be making a few tools with their machines. I need you to erase the recordings, of course."

The industrial fabrication plants were in the industrial sectors to the west of the academy. The streets in the area hummed and shook with the vibrations of machinery processing, pressing, and manufacturing. The industrial sector took up almost eighty percent of the power produced in the city. On Meridian, there was never any end to the transports arriving with raw materials and finished goods being pumped back out.

We arrived in a nondescript transport filled with a couple of block resources. Different chunks of materials we would use to refill the stock at the fabricator. Guards patrolled the outside of the building in force. We parked a distance from our target and walked in, watching for gaps.

"What makes this easy," began Remi as he drove us through the street and toward the factory, "are the protocols inside the building. Rent-a-guards don't have the clearance to see the innards of the fabrication plants, so we have to rely on a power outage to trick the sensors. Evelyn has been arranging *meetings* here for the past few days with a—well, let's call him a *gentleman*." He chuckled. "She used the opportunity to convince him to do a favor for her and sabotage the grid. We'll be able to slip in and out without a problem."

I struggled under the heavy bag of raw materials. It was far heavier than the usual gear bag for break-ins. Good thing I'd invested in myself with exercises on the track.

Remi was on his headset again, and I was safely concealed in my coat.

Guard patrols covered the area out to a 50-yard perimeter. It was a difficult jog with nearly 100 pounds of raw materials, but when Remi gave the signal I made a break for it and arrived at the building without being seen.

It was my first time working a clicker in the field. I had practiced on some test locks before, but there was always a difference from practice to actual application. The power dropped exactly when Evelyn said it would, though it took me longer than I would have liked to clear the door. Still, I managed to enter within the allotted time.

I waited inside the darkened factory for Remi's signal. It came seven minutes later—a few light knocks. I opened the door and he was in. He placed his bag next to mine and we made our way to the fabrication unit in question.

It took us another minute to link up a dummy terminal, which fed the necessary schematics to be fabricated into the machine.

Remi hit the activation sequence and pulled up a chair. "This could be a while. No reason we can't have a chat."

I took another seat and stretched my legs. "Do you know what we're building here?"

Remi smirked. "I thought you knew. This is all part of your plan, I'm told."

"What plan?" I asked.

Remi frowned. "C'mon, kid. All of this work you've been doing solving Evelyn's little puzzles? She's clearly pumping you for information to get free legwork out of you. I would complain, but it's good training."

I paused, quickly going over everything I had done so far with her. The first puzzle had been a test. She wanted to know how quickly I could come to a conclusion they had already found. From there, she had started putting me to tasks that she didn't have answers for but wanted to save time in finding. I ran back through the list in sequential order, trying to determine which of my solutions we might currently be using. After a few seconds, I returned my eyes to Remi. "You installed the cameras in the engineer's apartment?"

Remi nodded. "Yeah. That was good thinking, made my job low-risk."

"Do you know what she was working on?" I asked.

Remi shook his head. "No. I know she had a dozen degrees, so figuring out exactly what she might have been doing would only be a guess."

The process took just over three hours. When it was complete, we had three oddly shaped handles.

We made our way to the resource bin, took out the resource blocks, and inserted new ones according to the readout on the dummy terminal.

I was back in my room barely an hour later. We had just constructed the control mechanisms for the box in the complex.

THE NEXT DAY AT SCHOOL, I made a show of being depressed and angry in the hallway when I knew I would pass by Canton. I brooded my way through class, rarely volunteering answers but always offering the right ones when I did. He was increasingly watchful of me but didn't approach.

THE NEXT WEEK, Evelyn gathered us at Winston's place again. All of his furniture was gone, replaced by cheap but sturdy rentals. The apartment felt like a facade now, but it was far cleaner than it had been. I briefly wondered what Winston would think about the changes when he returned.

"Everything you've been doing up to now has been in preparation for a large-scale job," began Evelyn. "Sometime in the next few weeks, a shipment of neutronium will arrive at this facility and be held for approximately seventy-two hours before being processed. We need everything in place to capitalize on that window."

Remi, despite himself, leaned forward and took a step towards us. "Neutronium, you say? That's a big score. A *get-the-hell-off-the-planet-afterward* type of score."

Evelyn laughed. "Yes, Remi. Astute as always," she remarked. "You will be compensated enough from this single heist to set you up for several years, I would imagine. It will also be your final job with me. I'm sure you've trained

Alphonse adequately by now for the task ahead, so I remain confident in our ability to complete the project."

"What about the drilling?" I asked. "That alone will take weeks to do. If the neutronium shows up before we're done, we'll miss the window." I paused. "No, that's where Winston is. You've had him drilling this whole time."

Evelyn was pleased with herself. "He's a simple man. He doesn't mind being in a dank hole for days and days. I took the opportunity of his absence to redecorate. Do you think he'll like it?"

Remi scoffed. "No."

I shook my head. "I don't know that he'll care. So we still have several parts of the plan to get ready?"

Evelyn dropped her smile. "Fine. All business. I was expecting at least a kind word on the décor." She opened a box on the table and handed us each an earpiece. "Wear these at all times. When the shipment arrives, I will need to coordinate you into position quickly, no time to assemble. Alphonse, get yourself an excuse in place to leave class at a moment's notice."

We each took our earpiece and it buzzed in my ear as it calibrated. Afterward, I could barely feel it.

Remi worked his jaw in a circle a few times. "These things always make my ears pop. Years later and the pressure on this planet still screws with me. Put your tongue to the roof of your mouth to activate the transponder. Then whisper sub-vocally and it will transmit. Handy gizmos, but they burn out quickly."

Evelyn showed the contents of the box, where there was a dozen more. "You'll come back here each week for a fresh one until the job is done. As for tonight, Alphonse is correct, you are going to go cause problems with a financial office that handles the pensions for both the Union civilian maintenance workers and all the parts suppliers for the complex. One blow will cause issues with everything."

Remi smacked the side of his head and continued to work his jaw. He looked annoyed. "We doing this clean or pinning it on somebody?"

Evelyn stroked the fabric on the sofa and looked into the air. "I'm sure you will find somebody has been skimming once you get into the specifics. Might as well give credit where it's due."

———

Accessing the financial offices was easier than any previous job. While the elevator to the office floor was guarded from the lobby and used a keyed system for access, other floors were open with the press of a button. The building in question had a garden terrace restaurant. Traffic in the elevator and moving through the building was busy for late evening.

I went in plain clothes, but Remi stuck with his usual garb. He blended into the background easily, moving only when needed and not drawing attention to himself. We went up to the restaurant and requested a table before heading back, finally entering a restroom above the target floor and dropping down through an industrial duct system.

We slipped into the office from the restroom and surveyed the area, finding a dozen desks and workstations, an outer office for reception, and an inner office belonging to the company president. Remi got to work on opening the inner office while I started looking through desks.

Most of the workstations were easy to hack, though the president had attempted an extra layer of security on her own. Notes on other terminals indicated she had created a two-part passkey that had taken her staff hours to deal with whenever she wasn't in the office and they needed special approval. Apparently, the issue was so egregious that they had disabled the auto shut-off on her terminal several weeks ago, so it simply stopped locking. Great news for us, all things considered.

It took us thirty minutes to sift through the important files and reroute money from one company to another. It would take months for the affected businesses and personnel to detangle where the money had gone and why. We ran the initial and final transfers through the president's terminal, which would almost certainly cause the investigation team to cast blame on the office staff. With the well-documented undermining of her fastidious security protocols, they would likely be fired, which would slow down the recovery even more.

When our work was concluded, we retreated through the

ducts, back the way we came, making it in time for our reservation at the terrace restaurant.

I INTENSIFIED my attitude problem in class. I started wearing clothing I'd picked up that was worn and used. It was enough to have several teachers ask me to stay after class to confirm I wasn't having problems. I told them I was trying new things but always left it vague. The day before break, Canton finally approached me.

He sauntered up to me with a swagger that was a poor imitation of Vance's slouched walk, which flared an anger in me. "Alphonse, isn't it? Hey, you doing okay? Seems like things have been rough for you the last couple weeks."

I ignored him at first and trudged down the hall, intentionally looking at my feet.

He walked in front of me and stopped short so that I had to backpedal not to run into him. "I'm not here to rub it in. I want to help you."

I gave him a calculated look, one-part anger and one-part eager hope smothered under several parts of brooding. "I don't need help. It's fine."

He put his arm around me in another unwelcome imitation of Vance's behavior. "I know about you, y'know?"

I doubted that he knew anything more than rumors and the impressions I had spread myself. "You do?"

"Oh yeah. Look, it doesn't matter what you did to get tossed here. I see you working hard, trying to get through classes. It's tough when you don't have any outside funding coming in. Yeah, the academy gives you the basics, but who really can live on that? You need those premium perks to really put in the effort, right?"

I didn't respond.

He continued as if I had. "Yeah, you know. Well, I could help you out with that. I always have a little extra something I can spread around. It would be like a favor. Among friends."

I felt my skin crawl with his arm around me and his voice in my ear. "Really? I . . ." I let my voice trail. "No, no. I can't. I'm fine."

He hooked me a little tighter. "We both know that's a lie. Look, it doesn't have to be a favor. You don't have to owe me. Maybe you can do me a solid now and it won't even be a problem."

I brightened to that. "Yeah? I have some old clothes I can sell. Maybe a watch I've been holding on to."

He shook his head. "Nothing like that. You seem to be on top of things in bio, right? Like more than just on top."

There it was. The question I'd been waiting for.

I pretended to pull away. "I don't know what you're talking about."

He pulled me in tighter and dug his other hand into my ribs. "You know exactly what I'm talking about. Answering questions in class before the teacher can even finish asking. You never miss an answer. You're an amateur at this whole thing. You've got access to the answers, you gotta miss some of them or it's obvious. You're just lucky I caught on before the teachers did."

"Fine, I have a source," I said, reciting the script I had been rehearsing. "Some things Vance showed me. Look, I can't fail, and if I give you things, they'll know." I tried to sound panicked.

"It will be no problem. You get me the answers for the final, I slip you some cash after. You just make sure you answer more than a few wrong. Keep your score just above passing and nobody will know."

I again tried to push free and he relented. We were outside the science building now, so I turned like I was headed back to my room. "I'll get you what you need tomorrow. When can you get me the money?"

He laughed. "I'll need time to go over your work first. Don't worry about it. I'll see you get taken care of. Trust me. We're pals now." He smiled, and I forced myself to do the same.

He continued following me and we traveled to my room. I had a set of "answers" there that I had prepared in advance. He came into the room and I shuffled in my desk to bring out my pad and transfer the doctored file.

He grinned at me. "You'll see, Alphonse. This will be the best decision you ever made."

I smiled again. "I have no doubt about that."

THAT EVENING, the call came through the earpiece. For a moment, I thought I was thinking in Evelyn's voice.

"The shipment is on the way. We have barely over seventy-two hours to pull this off. Get off campus, and meet Remi in the shopping area downtown. You two need to sabotage the food truck tonight. Remi will have the contaminants. Now move."

I swapped out my disguise clothing for my heist wear and made my way off campus in a hurry.

Remi was already waiting in the parking area when I entered the shopping center. He popped out from behind a column as I entered the structure. "This way. I've got us a different kind of vehicle this time."

I followed him to the roof of the garage and saw that he had taken an ice cream truck from somewhere. "Isn't this conspicuous?"

He waved me inside. "The best way to hide is in plain sight. We're headed to a food packaging and catering company. This will let us slip right in."

We drove west to the southern end of the industrial area. As opposed to the heavy rumble of the central fabrication areas, the air here was filled with the not always appetizing smells of industrial food processing and production.

We pulled up to an entryway and stopped at the gate, then Remi leaned out the window to talk to the guy. "Hey, you were looking for a lost truck?"

The guard stared at the truck in confusion and then went through his records. "How did you know? Pull inside and get out of the truck. Don't make any sudden movements. I've got a team coming in to talk to you."

Remi pulled the truck in and then followed a pathway of lights to a loading dock. A group of four security guards was waiting there. He looked over to me. "How you feeling today, son?"

I grinned. "I'm good to back your play."

Remi nodded. "You're going to like this one. It's a classic from ancient literature."

Remi stopped the truck in the designated place. As soon as the engine powered down, our doors were pulled open and I was yanked out by a guard. We were brought around to the side and restrained. One guard stood by each of us while the other two started asking questions. "Where did you find this truck?"

"Me and my son saw it idling by a building downtown," Remi answered. "There was a drunk man inside. I've got him in the back."

The guards nodded to each other and made a series of hand gestures. They opened the back doors and found an unconscious man inside.

Remi interrupted before they could ask any other questions. "He looked like shit, so I put him in the back. I figured you'd miss the truck and could find out what was wrong with this guy."

The guards looked skeptical. "You did this out of kindness? Really?"

Remi balked at that. "No. I was kind of hoping you'd give

us a tour of the place. Maybe some samples? Me and the kid don't have a lot between us and I thought this would be a way we could see some decent eats."

Two guards pulled out the unconscious man and put him on a gurney that had been brought out. Another spoke into a commlink. "You two wait here." They walked away, leaving one guard with us.

We didn't have to wait long before a woman in a suit came out to greet us. "I apologize for the security staff. Missing vehicles don't just show up every day."

Remi laughed and shook hands with the woman after the guard lifted his restraints. "It is definitely weird. I understand."

The woman smiled. "You and your son wanted a tour?"

Remi nodded. "I thought I would show the boy how to act proper. Help out the companies and they'll help you, I told him."

I nodded. "Dad's always telling me that companies are good for us. It's just hard to believe since he's been out of work because they keep reducing—"

Remi cut me off. "Now, son. That's no talk for this lady. We're just happy to return the truck. If you are offering a tour, we'll take it; otherwise, we'll be on our way. We have to get to the shops if we want to scrounge up some dinner."

The woman was all smiles and apologies. "Think nothing of it. I'll give you a tour personally. If you will just follow me." She excused the guards.

Remi gave me a look. "Hey, son, make sure you grab our

packs from the truck." I looked in the back and there were two hiking backpacks. Lots of small pockets all around, they were well worn but fairly clean.

"I got 'em, Dad," I said, doing my best to dumb down my speech.

The tour lasted just over two hours. We managed to distract the woman back and forth and dumped a sample of contaminants in everything we could throughout the factory. There was going to be a lot of sick people in the future, but there was no way they would notice the problem at the complex as being out of the ordinary.

20

WE WAITED for the appropriate time window to enter the disused sewer, then took our position that night. Even with the excitement of the big job underway, I couldn't forget my other duties back at the academy. To avoid class, I listed myself as ill, making for a reasonable excuse. This was easily accepted, since I'd yet to fall sick even a single day. I could now focus on the job at hand.

Remi and I stalked through the dark tunnels of the disused sewer system following the map provided by the decades-old plans. This proved difficult going as many places had shifted in geologic activity. We had to make our way around numerous collapsed areas. The route was tight, but we were able to squeeze through them all with our portable containment box. The trip gave me some time to practice with the control handles, though I was told during exfiltration that job would fall to Winston.

When we arrived at the work area, Remi stopped me. "Winston? It's time. Let us in. It's Remington."

There was a silence in the dusty dark and then a small slash of light came out of a wall, followed by a soft beam. Winston, dirty and unwashed, waved to us from the other side of the baffle. He was as cheery as ever.

We entered the tunneling work space and I saw how Winston had been living for the past month. There was a waste bucket and spray in one corner. The rest of the space was occupied by a small cot and a mostly exhausted supply of water bottles and food ration boxes. Fuel cells littered the next chamber and the digging equipment proper.

Evelyn was right, Winston really didn't care where he lived. Prisons for captured soldiers offered more amenities and room. Remi set down his own gear bag and cleared out a space to sit. I powered down the containment unit and sat on the bed. It smelled of Winston in a way that I was not happy about.

Remi got everyone up to speed. "Winston, we make our move in fifteen hours. You have the tunnel complete?"

Winston continued to smile his innocent, broad grin. "I've been working really hard when the clock strikes like Evelyn said. There is less than an hour of drilling to go. I left that so we could enter and not be seen."

Remi nodded. "Alright. We wait until the window. From there, we punch through the wall and enter the facility. I'm on point. Alphonse, I need you sharp and ready to hand me gear as we work our way through. You have the patrols mapped out?"

I nodded.

"Good," said Remi. "You tell us when to start and stop. Winston, your job is to guide the containment box. You need to stay near us but don't crowd." He stretched and settled in for a nap on the floor. "If anything goes wrong *before* we get the box, we retreat to here and split. If anything goes wrong *after* we snag the goods, we make sure Alphonse gets out with it. No matter what that means."

I swallowed. Even with Remi's words hanging in the air, I figured that planning for success beat worrying about failure. Still, planning for all scenarios was wise, and Remi knew that.

Winston offered me the bed, but I declined and made myself semi comfortable on the remains of ration boxes on the floor. They were somewhat springy and smelled a lot less like three weeks without a wash.

We slept in small bursts whiling away the time. At one point, we played some cards to occupy ourselves in the dim light of a few lamps. We stayed quiet, partially out of the taciturn nature of the group but also in anticipation of the job.

Finally, the clock on Winston's nightstand beeped and we were ready. We dressed in our infiltration gear: combat-padded dark-colored clothing complete with face masks. Communication was through subvocal earpieces and there was even a several-minute air supply built into the face mask.

It was uncomfortable but offered some protection for the worst scenarios.

I took a last-minute itemization of the gear while Winston and Remi powered through the last of the wall separating us from the basement of the complex.

The wall gave way and we slipped in. Winston had done well. The tunnel took us into an electrical room in the basement. I handed Remi a remote shorted interchange and he attached it to the panel. Even as we installed the pinch, the power fluctuated. The internal power was already having issues. The pinch gave us the ability to manually trigger a rolling blackout to cover our movements, and the stressed engineering created an excuse to keep our actions from alarming the personnel.

With the pinch in place, I took a look at the time and counted out the patrols in my head. This was the biggest random factor with the plan. If the guards were less than professional, their patrol times could be compromised. I was counting on sick guards to maintain protocol but be bad at what they did. It was a contradiction that I felt strongly wouldn't be an issue. Dedication was a powerful motivator over time, but a poor motivator in the moment.

"Go."

Remi pushed through the door and I followed a second behind. Winston came up last and we threaded our way through a corridor to our first elevator. No alarms rang out as we entered and made our way to the second floor above ground.

As it arrived, I hit the remote for the pinch. The power went out and we sat in the elevator in the sallow yellow emergency lights. I counted out two minutes and it hit again. As soon as the power was back, Remi sent the elevator down to the first floor.

We exited to the left and ran to the end of the corridor, then we watched a patrol of guards head through a set of doors in front of us. The moment they were clear, we approached the door. It was a common Chrysalis door. I worked a sniffer on the panel to locate the code while Remi used a portable chromatograph to analyze the isotope. He then inserted a pack of quick-set resin into the hole.

The sniffer found the basic algorithm for the door and I waited to signal Remi. He gave me a thumbs-up that the resin was set.

"Now!" He turned the key in the window. The door's electronics allowed it to open and the makeshift key tripped the tumblers. The door opened, and we ran through and around another corner in time to see a new patrol entering from the end of the hallway.

From there, we entered the elevator and rode up to the fourth floor. Two more doors and we'd reached the next elevator. As we waited for a lift, an alarm sounded. I triggered the pinch and we held our breath as the power died and the backups tried to switch on. I hit the pinch again as they did, and the system reset a second time.

In theory, we were in the elevator and gone before anyone could figure out if we were real or a glitch.

That took us to the third floor and our target.

"Steady everyone," Remi said over the earpieces.

My heart was pounding and the rush of blood in my ears made the sound distant. For all my complaints about how the thrill of the prep mission was insufficient, this was almost too much.

We exited the elevator as a natural blackout struck. Remi and I were already out of the elevator, but the doors slammed shut automatically behind us. Winston shoved the containment unit through the door and dove forward. His foot got caught in the door. He turned red, containing a scream as the military-grade doors started to crush his foot.

Remi jumped at the door and fought for a tool on his harness. "Did you hit the pinch?" He jammed a strip of a red gummy substance on the upper section of the door. "Get back! Winston, pull!"

An explosion shoved the doors slightly apart and Winston freed his foot. The ceramic plating in the armor had cracked and splinters of it fell to the floor. He got to his feet and hobbled along.

Things were starting to go wrong. The sound also alerted a patrol. We could hear the pounding feet coming toward us. With no way to reenter the elevator and several bulkheads on standby, we were exposed.

"Any ideas?" Remi said.

I scoured through my mental map of the area. "Monitoring room, that door."

Remi had a clicker out before we got to the door and it

was open a moment later. We shoved the containment unit through and shut it behind us. Remi had his gun drawn in his other hand. The monitoring room could contain up to three technicians at any time but always had a minimum of one staff. Nobody was inside. We watched a warning light flick on the panel and a repeating video of us at the elevator. Remi cleared the footage and disabled the alert.

A voice echoed through a restroom door. "Hey, Carmichael? Did you find out what that alert was?" The voice was pained and stopped halfway through the sentence to deal with an evacuation out of one side or the other.

"It's fine," I called out. "Just more resets from the power."

"You okay? You sound muffled."

"I'm picking up something." I coughed. "I hope nobody else is getting it."

We watched through the monitor as a team of guards hit the elevator and inspected the area. One pointed to the scorched section of the door and another noticed the shards on the floor. A light blinked on the panel for an incoming message.

"Can you deal with that, Carmichael? I'm . . . ugh . . . going to need another minute."

I approached the console. "You got it." I hit the receiver. "What do you need?"

"This is patrol unit 7-Delta, you see what happened here?"

"Maintenance was working on the door when the power

came offline. Slammed shut and broke a tool. Nearly tore his hand off. I've got him in here for basic care."

"Does he need an escort out?"

"Negative. He's fine, just spooked. Soon as the power is back on, we'll get the hall cleared."

"Sounds good. 7-Delta out."

We waited for the group to clear the hallway and continued along our way. The power kicked back on as we approached the final hallway to our destination.

One more Chrysalis door and we were in the antechamber. From here, we had no way of knowing what the vault door to the actual box would be like. No amount of digging revealed what that was made of or how it was accessed.

Remi lined the edges with more of the red gummy substance he had. "Everyone back. We're blowing this and then finding the fastest way out. Alphonse, the moment I hit it, we need to knock out the power. Got it?"

"Copy. Ready when you are."

He stepped back to the edge of the room and pushed us behind him. "Mark."

The vault door fizzled for a brief moment as I hit the pinch. The lights went off, but it remained bright in the room as the explosive seared the edges of the vault door. It burned white hot and I shut my eyes for a few long seconds. When I opened them again, my vision was still splotchy.

The door fell inward, smashing into a staging table. A leg of the table slammed me in the side of the head. I went down tasting copper and feeling dizzy. Remi moved to help me, but

I waved him off. "Nothing broken," I managed to say. "Get the stuff."

Winston navigated the containment unit into the vault and moved it into position. He and Remi pulled on protective gloves and together the two pulled several containers out of the larger vault storage unit and fitted them into the portable one. The power came on again and an alarm was ringing. I hit the pinch and nothing happened.

"Remi, I'm getting nothing from the pinch."

"Don't worry yet. The interference in the vault and the explosion could have scrambled it. Proceed as normal. Let's move!"

They came out of the vault and we formed up again, this time with Remi at point and me taking up a position behind Winston and the containment unit.

As we entered the hallway, I saw that we were in trouble. The lights were all on and alarms were blaring. I hit the pinch a few times and got no response. Worse, the bulkheads had come down in front of us.

Remi paced in front of the door. It seemed like we had come so far only to be trapped. We had only three options. Try to get through the doors back the way we came, which was slow and we were limited on the materials for defeating the isotope locks. We could go back to the vault, which was pointless. Or we could divert our route further into the complex.

I explained the options to Remi.

"Is there any route out if we go further in?" he asked.

229

"It goes into some of the third-wave upgrades," I said. "So I don't know what we'll face, but there is a route that gets us back to the basement."

Remi nodded. "Let's move."

We continued down the hallway and accessed an elevator, which took us up to the fifth floor. The elevator opened and we found ourselves in a dark hallway. The power outages seemed to be contained to this floor only as the elevator was still working on a redundancy.

We moved to the next intersection and found a closed bulkhead door. Remi swore and dropped into a combat firing stance. "This is where we start into the at-all-costs plan. No other way."

I noticed that the door blocking our way was one of the new Chrysalis prototypes. "I think we're okay. I can get us through this."

Remi frowned as I pulled out the device. "I told you to get rid of that thing. No telling what tracers or backdoors are in it. Dammit, kid."

The power came back on and I pressed my thumb and pinky on the pad. The door opened. "You can yell at me later. Right now, this is our way out."

We broke into a run then, staying just in front of another patrol. We worked our way to the elevator and back down to the second floor. From there, we only had to work through one more hallway to the first elevator. Alarms rang out again and an all-units was called on the vault. We only had to wait for the halls to clear before I opened the last door between us and the elevator. We were down and out into the tunnel in under five minutes.

We had done it.

We moved the containment unit to Winston's Klemtite company transport and made our way to a warehouse location. Evelyn was waiting for us. She gave us a flirty wave as we opened the transport and brought out the containment unit.

"Oh my, look at this. My three favorite people and the box of my dreams. Well done, everyone. Now open it up, let me check the goods."

Winston pulled the lid off the unit and Remi handed her a pair of protective gloves. We stood back as she carefully lifted and inspected each canister.

"All of our dreams are coming true now. We'll split up and return here in two days. That will be enough time for the majority of the heat to die down. I have a buyer lined up that will meet us then. Now everyone get home and get some rest." She seemed to actually notice us for the first time since seeing the box. "Especially you, Winston. Go take showers until the meet. Yeech."

She didn't seem to notice the way he limped or the way I tilted my head. Still, when it came to a score this big, anyone could get dizzied by the numbers.

21

REMI DROPPED me off a block from the academy's fence line, allowing me to sneak back inside. Before he let me out, he took a moment to give me a once-over. "Looks like you got clipped pretty good. That is why we wear armor into a job like that. Without the helmet and goggles, you could have suffered a fracture. Solid pupil response, so I don't suspect a concussion. It will bruise up, but you'll be fine. You got an excuse to cover this shit when you get to class?"

I grinned and grimaced a bit with the pain of the action. "I have something in place, yeah."

He let me out of the transport and drove off.

I entered campus and snuck into my room through the recently fixed external hallway door. Nobody saw me enter.

I sent a message to Manson and Gil. *You will both be called into the headmaster's tomorrow. No matter what, just agree that you saw*

Canton do it. Add no details and offer no reasons. Just repeat those words and you'll be front row for what happens after.

Only one thing left to do, and Canton would be dealt with. I checked myself in the mirror before going to sleep. It looked like I had been clubbed severely on the one side. Despite the pain, I didn't apply ice or take anything. I needed to look as terrible as I could for the next part.

Even with the pain, it was easy to sleep. I was exhausted from the adrenaline rush of the job and the promise of action the following day.

I AWOKE the next day and intentionally missed my first few classes. By midday, Maevik was at the door. "Alphonse? You gave yourself a sick note yesterday, but we haven't heard anything. If you don't open the door, I'm authorized to enter. Please open up."

I stumbled to the door in my underclothes and opened it. I hadn't showered from the heavy equipment and the night in the tunnel. I played up the pain as best I could. Given her past as a field medic, my injuries wouldn't hold up to much scrutiny if I overdid it.

She sat me on the bed and flashed a light in my eyes. "What happened to you? Who did this to you?"

I acted confused and embarrassed. "I can't say. Just tell them I'm ill and need a few days. Please?"

She shook her head. "I'm not going to let this go. Some-body attacked you. You have to tell me who."

I put up one more attempt. "I don't want trouble. Just let it go, I'll be fine."

She pulled me from the bed and shook me a bit. "Alphonse, I can't let you sit here like this."

Now for the hard part. I looked her in the eye. "Give me a minute to get dressed, then I need you to escort me to Head-master Whiles. I'll tell him everything."

She nodded and took a step back, realizing for the first time that I was barely dressed. "Alright. I'll be outside. You have a minute, then I'm right back in here. One minute."

The door closed and I got dressed in a hurry. There was no pushing the matter further now. I opened the door and Maevik walked me to the headmaster's office. Classes were in session, so nobody saw me enter. Maevik sat me down and talked to the assistant and then ushered me into the headmas-ter's office. I didn't say a word the whole time.

Headmaster Whiles gasped in shock when he saw me. "Oh my. This is worse than I thought. You said injury. I didn't expect this level of assault. Alphonse, who did this to you?"

I looked at the clock. The bio final was just starting. I suppressed a smirk and looked at the headmaster with my best approximation of fear and worry. "It's about this." I turned on my data pad and transferred the fake test answers to him. "The student—and I'm not naming anyone—that answers the bio final with these answers threatened me. He'd hurt me if I didn't give him the answers." I summoned a few tears and a choked a little. "I gave him fake answers and he's going to be so mad when he finds out. Check the tests and do something. Don't let him hurt me. I said nothing."

I hid my face in my hands and sobbed the best I could. The headmaster stepped out with Maevik. I could hear them talking about solutions and evidence and so on. I overheard them mention Manson and Gil. Everything was ready now.

Manson and Gil were brought into the office. They took a look at me and the moment they saw my face they both started yelling.

"Canton did it!" said Manson, jamming an oversized pudgy finger at me. "I saw him."

Gil chimed in. "It was out back of the dorms. Canton did it."

I used my frustration with their adlibs to get in an extra painful sob.

Headmaster Whiles sent for Mr. Aldwell, the bio teacher, and Canton. Gil and Manson sat next to me and I whispered to them, "Just stay quiet and let it happen from here."

They nodded, forgetting that they were supposed to be subtle.

Mr. Aldwell came in next.

"Do you have the record of the test answers for today's final?" Whiles asked.

Aldwell admitted he did. "I've just sent them to your pad. I didn't see anyone doing anything in the test. The only abnormal thing was the absence of Alphonse for the second day in a row." He saw me then and also gasped. "I see. Well. Nothing unusual, then."

Canton came in next. He gave me a look and then moved on to Manson and Gil. He reacted immediately. "They're lying. Whatever they say, they got no proof. No way I did any of it."

Headmaster Whiles projected the comparison between the fake answers I gave and Canton's test results. "Why are you the only student who answered every question wrong and also answered every question identically to this forged answer sheet?"

Canton glared at the headmaster then at me. "You? You'll pay for this. My father is a powerful man. You won't get away with any of it."

Maevik grabbed Canton and kept him from lunging at me.

Manson and Gil started shouting. "We all know it was you. You're out of excuses."

Maevik dragged him out of the office and restrained him.

Headmaster Whiles shook his head. "I'm sorry, Canton. With evidence like this, I have no choice but to immediately remove you from Quintell Academy. You will be put on a transport and your parents contacted. As this is the end of the term, it is unlikely you will be allowed to finish. That will be dealt with by your new school."

Canton fought through a few different emotions. He was angry and confused and scared. The bottom had just dropped out of his whole world. Everything he thought about himself was slipping away.

Standing where he could see me, I slouched against the wall and gave him my best Vance impression, then I winked.

I SPENT the rest of that day at the clinic getting cleaned up. They confirmed it was just a bruise and no hairline fracture or concussion, then they gave me some anti-inflammatory meds for the swelling. I returned to my room, and the following day I was excused from classes to avoid any revenge plots from Canton's friends and associates. They probably also wanted to hide my face from the rest of the students. I used the time to catch up on the work of the last few days.

I had time to rest before the meet later in the day. All in all, I felt great. We had pulled off a lucrative heist without getting caught, hurting anyone, or losing anyone. I had sealed Canton's fate and gotten revenge for Vance.

I thought about what that meant now, in the aftermath. What did I do now that I had succeeded at everything I had set out to do? These thoughts kept me occupied until I snuck out of campus and headed to the meet.

I TOOK a transport to a restaurant a few blocks from the meet and then walked over. Traveling inconspicuously was difficult when you couldn't drive. If I was going to keep up this business, I would need to solve the question of transportation.

I walked into the abandoned warehouse and made my way to the meeting room. I entered to see Remi already inside, posted up against a wall and eyeing me, as always. Winston was sitting on a box next to what I assumed was the containment unit covered in tarps and sheets.

I didn't see Evelyn.

Remi gave me a nod. "Any word?"

"Just me. I didn't see any transports outside. Winston, did you come with Evelyn?"

Winston stared at his hands and seemed disconnected from the room. He looked up. "She said she'd be late. She was having a drink with someone important. She likes to have drinks with important people."

I nodded. That sounded typical except that she was always on time to meetings that she set.

Remi popped off the wall, gun in hand. I saw the movement and then heard a trio of boots pounding their way through the warehouse.

Three Union officers came in behind me, guns drawn. I stumbled backward and landed near Remi's feet. "You're under arrest for crimes against the Union and its citizens. Get down now!"

"Like hell!" Remi opened fire. The two on the right and center dropped as his shots cut straight through their armor. The one on the left managed to dodge to the side and get behind a pillar. I was scrambling to figure out what had just happened, while Winston held his hands over his ears and ducked down.

Remi scanned for the third officer.

Another set of shots rang out and I felt Remi go down almost on top of me. The officer came out from behind the pillar and leveled the gun. "Don't move!"

I froze. Remi's gun was straight ahead and still smoking from the discharged rounds.

Winston stood up and screamed. The officer pivoted toward him and I took the opportunity.

I scooped up the weapon and fired three times. The first missed, far to the right. The second landed in the center of the officer's chest. The third clipped through the top of his shoulder.

He dropped, a hard smack as his helmet hit the floor.

I stared at him for longer than I knew before finally swallowing. I tightened my shaking hands, clenching my fingers as I tried to steady myself. "Are you alright, Winston?"

I turned to him, only to find him running toward me. Winston wrapped his arms around me and began carrying me away from the warzone.

"E says I should leave now," he told me as he held onto me. "I have to leave, Alphonse. Have to kill you quick."

It only took me a moment to see the earpiece. He must have been in communication with his sister the entire time. "W-Wait, Winston—" I tried to angle my mouth away from his chest. "What are you doing?"

He wrapped his hands around my neck and squeezed. "E

says I have to, Alphonse. I don't want to, but she says you can't come. Sorry."

"W-What?" I asked.

His arms tightened around me and I struggled to breathe, virtually powerless against the large simpleton. My head whirled and I could barely see past the red splotches in my vision. As I lost the sensation in my cheeks, my neck, and my shoulders, something in me flared—a deep fear that I could not resist, and I fired another set of shots, no thought to it at all.

The gun clicked on the third round.

The pressure on my throat eased up and I took a few haggard breaths before managing to wiggle my way free.

Winston's hands went to his shoulder. There was blood from where I'd shot him.

The giant groaned, all his attention diverted to his wound. I regained myself and, wavering on my feet, managed to pull out his earpiece.

I shuffled away from him and put the comm in my ear, working my jaw for a moment, trying to get it to engage. "Evelyn?"

"Oh, Alphonse. Did you survive?" she asked. "Where's my brother?"

I ignored the question, quickly turning over the situation in my head and readjusting myself. A few seconds later, I cleared my throat. "So, you're taking the prize for yourself."

"Of course, I am. Did you think I would really split this

fortune with a Renegade and a student? Please. My plans are too grand for that."

The world was spinning in more ways than one. "I'll find you."

"Alphonse, I'm already off-planet with my prize. You, on the other hand, will either be in a cell or dead by the end of the night. You might want to start running."

"Evelyn, you don't get to just walk away from this. I won't allow—"

She laughed. "Go away now, boy."

The line went dead.

"Evelyn? Evelyn!" I barked.

I could hear sirens nearby. Even if I wanted to run, there was nowhere to go.

A grunt came from nearby. It was Remi, blinking on the ground. I ran to him, quickly ripping a piece of cloth from his shirt and pressing it into the open gunshot wound to apply pressure. "How many fingers am I holding up?" I asked. "Can you hear my voice?"

He reached a hand into the air and I grabbed it. "Did the bitch fuck us?" he asked, a garble in his throat. "I should've known better than to trust her. The cute ones always—"

"Hold on, Remi. They'll be here to arrest us, but they'll give you medical attention. Just be still," I told him, the words falling out of me.

"Hey, kid," he said, reaching for my hand. "Give me my gun."

"What?" I asked, looking down at the weapon.

"It's proper to die with your gun," he muttered, then gave me a knowing look. "And you can't be holding it when they get here."

"But, you—"

"I'm tired," he said, his eyes dropping a little. "Wish I had a pillow."

I shoved the gun into his hand. "Just hold on."

"Be good, Alphonse," he said, his tired eyes drifting as he lost sight of me. "Be better than me."

EPILOGUE

I sat in a dark room with a single overhead light.

I should have seen this coming.

All that time spent thinking about how to present myself, what other people did or thought, and how I ought to be. I was attentive, saw all the things that no one else could see.

But I didn't see this.

I thought about every interaction I'd had with Evelyn and how she had manipulated me.

A voice came through a speaker somewhere at the periphery of the darkness. "Prisoner, you will be moved shortly. Remain where you are."

I sat in the dark for a long time.

FOUR DAYS LATER, guards came to my cell. It was, as I'd imagined, bigger than the space that Winston lived in for a month digging that tunnel. It was about the same size as my dorm room with many of the same amenities. Prison and school were only different in what produced the stretches of boredom.

The guard banged on my door. "Prisoner! Hands!"

I put my hands through the slat in the middle of the door and felt shackles snapping into place. The door opened and I was escorted through the hallways and into a small white room. It was neutrally lit and almost pleasant in comparison to the gray industrial décor of the rest of the prison. A man I recognized was already seated inside.

The guard opened the door and sat me down. He shackled my hands to the table and turned to the man. "I'll be right outside." Then he left and we were alone.

The man was old, whip thin, and dressed in an immaculate suit. I had met him once as Mr. Black the day before my transfer to Quintell.

He smiled at me. "Hello again, Mr. Malloy. Nice to see you. I'm Malcolm Shaw."

I shrugged. The action sent ripples of pain through my fractured eye socket and bruised face. Winston might have been impressed to know that the injury he'd given me still ached. I wondered where he was right now.

"That's one lie you've admitted to," I said. "So much for Mr. Black."

Shaw smiled. "Yes, well, that was part of the job. I'm sure you understand."

"What brings you here today?" I asked, getting straight to the point. "Sending me to another school?"

The old man laughed. "We'll see about that," he said. "I heard reports about the activities you and your cohorts have been up to. I was rather surprised when I heard one of Evelyn's accomplices was still alive. Actually, two. We picked up the brother. He corroborated much of your story. Of course, he begged for a deal. For an idiot, he certainly knew his rights."

I watched the man carefully, as I had in the headmaster's office months ago.

"We know you came up with the plan that successfully thwarted our security and led to the theft of the neutronium," he said. "Some people used the word *mastermind* when describing that type of position. What nobody can seem to figure out is why you did it. A well-mannered student with exceptional grades and a bright future, plenty of money in their personal account. Care to explain?"

I remained silent.

"You didn't need the money," he went on. "You had nobody to benefit with your actions. You, as far as we know, don't have a cause to fight for. Why did you do it? What did you hope to gain?"

I considered the answers I had been preparing to his original question about the future. The way that Vance and Remi talked about shaping a world through action. Making choices.

I had never longed for any of those things. Not when it all came down to it. Not when I reflected on my choices. I'd spent the last few days in a cell with nothing but my thoughts to keep me company, and in that time, I had found solitude to be a powerful incentive for reflection.

"I did it for the puzzles," I answered, knowing as I said the words that it was the truth. "I wanted to beat the challenges Evelyn presented. I wanted to let Canton know that he couldn't get away with something because he had power or influence. I wanted to show everyone that I saw through them. That I knew things about them. That the truth was there, I only had to look. I wanted to prove that I shaped the world around me with that truth."

Shaw leaned forward in his chair. "I saw something in you back at the school. It was the second time your name had come across my desk. You have an intuitive nature for figuring people out but no discipline. I sent you to Quintell to keep an eye on you. And in three months, you both thwarted and exceeded my expectations. I had hoped to use you to expose Evelyn's scheme, but you ended up instrumental in its execution."

I said nothing.

His eyes lingered on me for a long moment, and like Evelyn before him, I could not tell what this man was thinking. He pulled out a card and slid it across the table to me, then flipped it over. The card had a strange symbol on it—an upside-down triangle with a circle inside and a line running through it. "Have you heard of the Constable Program, Alphonse?" the old man finally asked.

The question caught me by surprise, and I stared at the card, searching my memory for it. I had seen it in places, including news reports and different books regarding the Union and certain military exploits across the galaxy, but never had I made the connection. Never had I found the word Constable anywhere near it. "I know it exists," I said, recalling an article I had come across, perhaps six months back, and a few vague references to the program itself. "I understand that the Constables are a powerful arm of the Union's military, though their exploits are high classified. Nobody can say for certain who they are or specifically what they do."

Shaw smiled again. "Astute and spoken with the same blunt charm as everything you say. I know you can deceive and conceal that charm when you want. I saw you do so with Canton."

"It was for the truth."

Shaw chuckled. "Indeed. The Constables are intelligence officers of the Union. They have access to information and resources beyond what you may imagine. They work to unravel mysteries and plots with staggering consequences and unparalleled difficulty. They solve puzzles, in short."

I leaned forward. "I knew you weren't a school administrator."

"Did you, now?" he asked with a half-smile.

"I *suspected* there was a lie in play but couldn't see how to get to the truth. I just didn't know how I knew it." I paused. "It's always been that way."

Shaw was quiet for a moment, eyeing me with a look of cold examination. "You have talent, Alphonse. A natural ability that goes beyond that of most others." He paused again. "But you lack the training to understand it."

I considered the point. "How do I know any of it?"

"You see things you aren't fully cognizant of. People behave in many ways, from the acute to the obtuse. You read into their layers and come up with precise conclusions. Micro-expressions, behaviors, word choice—tiny pieces added up to form a person. Through this, you can see their true selves, their lies, their falsehoods. It is a rare gift, and it is something that the Constables know all too well."

I said nothing, not certain of how to even react. Here was a man like me, I realized, and he had been since the start.

He walked behind me and placed a hand on my shoulder. "You have more raw instinct than many agents have after years of training. Think of how much farther you could reach if you learn intentionally. If you are guided and challenged."

I tried to ignore the unfamiliar touch and kept staring straight ahead. "You think I can learn all of that? What would be the point?"

Shaw let go of my shoulder and walked back to the other side of the table. "You don't have to care about the fate of the Union. You don't have to care about yourself. But I know that you care about people. Your actions in protecting Manson and Gil, your revenge for Vance's expulsion, the way you refused to blackmail Whiles. Causes are not important to you, that's fine. Causes are nothing but aggregations of people in motion. As long as you care about people, the Union has a use for you. I have a use for you."

I considered the pitch and made a decision. "Remi's family didn't deserve the Union. If I help, I want two things."

Shaw brightened. "I love a bargain established from an uneven position. What do you have for me?"

"I want to see Evelyn answer for what she's done. I promised her that. I also want your assurances that if I find any corruption within the Union, you'll help me put an end to it."

Shaw replied without missing a beat. "Evelyn will be found," he said, no doubt in his voice. "She'll leave a trail and we will follow, rest assured. As for your second request, if you ever happened upon corruption and didn't speak out about it, I would be remiss to think you are the person I see before me now." He smiled. "And I'm so rarely wrong."

"Good," I remarked. "What now?"

"Learn and train," he told me. "Become a Constable."

"I'll do it," I said, a rising heat in my chest as I spoke the words.

"Of that, I have no doubt," he said, standing to his feet. "But it will take time, Alphonse, and there is still so much that you must learn."

PREVIEW: THE AMBER PROJECT

Documents of Historical, Scientific, and
*   Cultural Significance*
Play Audio Transmission File 021
Recorded April 19, 2157

CARTWRIGHT: *This is Lieutenant Colonel Felix Cartwright. It's been a week since my last transmission and two months since the day we found the city…the day the world fell apart. If anyone can hear this, please respond.*

If you're out there, no doubt you know about the gas. You might think you're all that's left. But if you're receiving this, let me assure you, you are not alone. There are people here. Hundreds, in fact, and for now, we're safe. If you can make it here, you will be, too.

The city's a few miles underground, not far from El Rico Air Force

Base. That's where my people came from. As always, the coordinates are attached. If anyone gets this, please respond. Let us know you're there… that you're still alive.

End Audio File

April 14, 2339
Maternity District

MILES BELOW THE SURFACE OF THE EARTH, deep within the walls of the last human city, a little boy named Terry played quietly with his sister in a small two-bedroom apartment.

Today was his very first birthday. He was turning seven.

"What's a birthday?" his sister Janice asked, tugging at his shirt. She was only four years old and had recently taken to following her big brother everywhere he went. "What does it mean?"

Terry smiled, eager to explain. "Mom says when you turn seven, you get a birthday. It means you grow up and get to start school. It's a pretty big deal."

"When will I get a birthday?"

"You're only four, so you have to wait."

"I wish I was seven," she said softly, her thin black hair hanging over her eyes. "I want to go with you."

He got to his feet and began putting the toy blocks away. They had built a castle together on the floor, but Mother would yell if they left a mess. "I'll tell you all about it when I get home. I promise, okay?"

"Okay!" she said cheerily and proceeded to help.

Right at that moment, the speaker next to the door let out a soft chime, followed by their mother's voice. "Downstairs, children," she said. "Hurry up now."

Terry took his sister's hand. "Come on, Jan," he said.

She frowned, squeezing his fingers. "Okay."

They arrived downstairs, their mother nowhere to be found.

"She's in the kitchen," Janice said, pointing at the farthest wall. "See the light-box?"

Terry looked at the locator board, although his sister's name for it worked just as well. It was a map of the entire apartment, with small lights going on and off in different colors, depending on which person was in which room. *There's us*, he thought, *green for me and blue for Janice, and there's Mother in red*. Terry never understood why they needed something like that because of how small the apartment was, but every family got one, or so Mother had said.

As he entered the kitchen, his mother stood at the far counter sorting through some data on her pad. "What's that?" he asked.

"Something for work," she said. She tapped the front of the pad and placed it in her bag. "Come on, Terrance, we've got to get you ready and out the door. Today's your first day, after all, and we have to make a good impression."

"When will he be back?" asked Janice.

"Hurry up. Let's go, Terrance," she said, ignoring the question. She grabbed his hand and pulled him along. "We have about twenty minutes to get all the way to the education district. Hardly enough time at all." Her voice was sour. He had noticed it more and more lately, as the weeks went on, ever since a few months ago when that man from the school came to visit. His name was Mr. Huxley, one of the few men who Terry ever had the chance to talk to, and from the way Mother acted—she was so agitated—he must have been important.

"Terrance." His mother's voice pulled him back. "Stop moping and let's go."

Janice ran and hugged him, wrapping her little arms as far around him as she could. "Love you," she said.

"Love you too."

"Bye," she said shyly.

He kissed her forehead and walked to the door, where his mother stood talking with the babysitter, Ms. Cartwright. "I'll only be a few hours," Mother said. "If it takes any longer, I'll message you."

"Don't worry about a thing, Mara," Ms. Cartwright assured her. "You take all the time you need."

Mother turned to him. "There you are," she said, taking his hand. "Come on, or we'll be late."

As they left the apartment, Mother's hand tugging him along, Terry tried to imagine what might happen at school today. Would it be like his home lessons? Would he be behind the other children, or was everything new? He enjoyed learning, but there was still a chance the school might be too hard for him. What would he do? Mother had taught him some things, like algebra and English, but who knew how far along the other kids were by now?

Terry walked quietly down the overcrowded corridors with an empty, troubled head. He hated this part of the district. So many people on the move, brushing against him, like clothes in an overstuffed closet.

He raised his head, nearly running into a woman and her baby. She had wrapped the child in a green and brown cloth, securing it against her chest. "Excuse me," he said, but the lady ignored him.

His mother paused and looked around. "Terrance, what are you doing? I'm over here," she said, spotting him.

"Sorry."

They waited together for the train, which was running a few minutes behind today.

"I wish they'd hurry up," said a nearby lady. She was young, about fifteen years old. "Do you think it's because of the outbreak?"

"Of course," said a much older woman. "Some of the trains are busy carrying contractors to the slums to patch the walls. It slows the others down because now they have to make more stops."

"I heard fourteen workers died. Is it true?"

"You know how the gas is," she said. "It's very quick. Thank God for the quarantine barriers."

Suddenly, there was a loud smashing sound, followed by

three long beeps. It echoed through the platform for a moment, vibrating along the walls until it was gone. Terry flinched, squeezing his mother's hand.

"Ouch," she said. "Terrance, relax."

"But the sound," he said.

"It's the contractors over there." She pointed to the other side of the tracks, far away from them. It took a moment for Terry to spot them, but once he did, it felt obvious. Four of them stood together. Their clothes were orange, with no clear distinction between their shirts and their pants, and on each of their heads was a solid red plastic hat. Three of them were holding tools, huddled against a distant wall. They were reaching inside of it, exchanging tools every once in a while, until eventually the fourth one called them to back away. As they made some room, steam rose from the hole, with a puddle of dark liquid forming at the base. The fourth contractor handled a machine several feet from the others, which had three legs and rose to his chest. He waved the other four to stand near him and pressed the pad on the machine. Together, the contractors watched as the device flashed a series of small bright lights. It only lasted a few seconds. Once it was over, they gathered close to the wall again and resumed their work.

"What are they doing?" Terry asked.

His mother looked down at him. "What? Oh, they're fixing the wall, that's all."

"Why?" he asked.

"Probably because there was a shift last night. Remember when the ground shook?"

Yeah, I remember, he thought. *It woke me up.* "So they're fixing it?"

"Yes, right." She sighed and looked around. "Where is that damned train?"

Terry tugged on her hand. "That lady over there said it's late because of the gas."

His mother looked at him. "What did you say?"

"The lady...the one right there." He pointed to the younger girl a few feet away. "She said the gas came, so that's why the trains are slow. It's because of the slums." He paused a minute. "No, wait. It's because they're *going* to the slums."

His mother stared at the girl, turning back to the tracks and saying nothing.

"Mother?" he said.

"Be quiet for a moment, Terrance."

Terry wanted to ask her what was wrong, or if he had done anything to upset her, but he knew when to stay silent. So he left it alone like she wanted. Just like a good little boy.

The sound of the arriving train filled the platform with such horrific noise that it made Terry's ears hurt. The train, still vibrating as he stepped onboard, felt like it was alive.

After a short moment, the doors closed. The train was moving.

Terry didn't know if the shaking was normal or not. Mother had taken him up to the medical wards on this train once when he was younger, but never again after that. He didn't remember much about it, except that he liked it. The medical wards were pretty close to where he lived, a few stops before the labs, and several stops before the education district. After that, the train ran through Pepper Plaza, then the food farms and Housing Districts 04 through 07 and finally the outer ring factories and the farms. As Terry stared at the route map on the side of the train wall, memorizing what he could of it, he tried to imagine all the places he could go and the things he might see. What kind of shops did the shopping plaza have, for example, and what was it like to work on the farms? Maybe one day he could go and find out for himself— ride the train all day to see everything there was to see. Boy, wouldn't that be something?

"Departure call: 22-10, education district," erupted the com in its monotone voice. It took only a moment before the train began to slow.

"That's us. Come on," said Mother. She grasped his hand, pulling him through the doors before they were fully opened.

Almost to the school, Terry thought. He felt warm suddenly. Was he getting nervous? And why now? He'd known about this forever, and it was only hitting him *now*?

He kept taking shorter breaths. He wanted to pull away and return home, but Mother's grasp was tight and firm, and the closer they got to the only major building in the area, the tighter and firmer it became.

Now that he was there, now that the time had finally come, a dozen questions ran through Terry's mind. Would the other kids like him? What if he wasn't as smart as everyone else? Would they make fun of him? He had no idea what to expect.

Terry swallowed, the lump in his throat nearly choking him.

An older man stood at the gate of the school's entrance. He dressed in an outfit that didn't resemble any of the clothes in Terry's district or even on the trains. A gray uniform—the color of the pavement, the walls, and the streets—matched his silver hair to the point where it was difficult to tell where one ended and the other began. "Ah," he said. "Mara, I see you've brought another student. I was wondering when we'd meet the next one. Glad to see you're still producing. It's been, what? Five or six years? Something like that, I think."

"Yes, thank you, this is Terrance," said Mother quickly. "I was told there would be an escort." She paused, glancing over the man and through the windows. "Where's Bishop? He assured me he'd be here for this."

"The *colonel*," he corrected, "is in his office, and the boy is to be taken directly to him as soon as I have registered his arrival."

She let out a frustrated sigh. "He was supposed to meet me at the gate for this himself. I wanted to talk to him about a few things."

"What's wrong?" Terry asked.

She looked down at him. "Oh, it's nothing, don't worry. You have to go inside now, that's all."

"You're not coming in?"

"I'm afraid not," said the man. "She's not permitted."

"It's all right," Mother said, cupping her hand over his cheek. "They'll take care of you in there."

But it's just school, Terry thought. "I'll see you tonight, though, right?"

She bent down and embraced him tightly, more than she had in a long time. He couldn't help but relax. "I'm sorry, Terrance. Please be careful up there. I know you don't understand it now, but you will eventually. Everything will be fine." She rose, releasing his hand for the first time since they left the train. "So that's it?" Mother said to the man.

"Yes, ma'am."

"Good." She turned and walked away, pausing a moment as she reached the corner and continued until she was out of sight.

The man pulled out a board with a piece of paper on it. "When you go through here, head straight to the back of the hall. A guard there will take you to see Colonel Bishop. Just do what they say and answer everything with either 'Yes, sir' or 'No, sir,' and you'll be fine. Understand?"

Terry didn't understand, but he nodded anyway.

The man pushed open the door with his arm and leg, holding it there and waiting. "Right through here you go," he said.

Terry entered, reluctantly, and the door closed quickly behind him.

The building, full of the same metal and shades of brown and gray that held together the rest of the city, rose higher than any other building Terry had ever been in. Around the room, perched walkways circled the walls, cluttered with doors and hallways that branched off into unknown regions. Along the walkways, dozens of people walked back and forth as busily as they had in the train station. More importantly, Terry quickly realized, most of them were men.

For so long, the only men he had seen were the maintenance workers who came and went or the occasional teacher who visited the children when they were nearing their birthdays. It was so rare to see any men at all, especially in such great numbers. *Maybe they're all teachers*, he thought. They weren't dressed like the workers: white coats and some with brown jackets—thick jackets with laced boots and bodies as stiff as the walls. Maybe that was what teachers wore. How could he know? He had never met one besides Mr. Huxley, and that was months ago.

"Well, don't just stand there gawking," said a voice from the other end of the room. It was another man, dressed the same as the others. "Go on in through here." He pointed to another door, smaller than the one Terry had entered from. "Everyone today gets to meet the colonel. Go on now. Hurry up. You don't want to keep him waiting."

Terry did as the man said and stepped through the doorway, his footsteps clanking against the hard metal floor, echoing through what sounded like the entire building.

"Well, come in, why don't you?" came a voice from inside.

Terry stepped cautiously into the room, which was much nicer than the entranceway. It was clean, at least compared to some of the other places Terry had been, including his own home. The walls held several shelves, none of which lacked for any company of things. Various ornaments caught Terry's eye, like the little see-through globe on the shelf nearest to the door, which held a picture of a woman's face inside, although some of it was faded and hard to make out. There was also a crack in it. What purpose could such a thing have? Terry couldn't begin to guess. Next to it lay a frame with a small, round piece of metal inside of it. An inscription below the glass read, "U.S. Silver Dollar, circa 2064." Terry could easily read the words, but he didn't understand them. What was this thing? And why was it so important that it needed to be placed on a shelf for everyone to look at?

"I said come in," said Bishop abruptly. He sat at the far end of the room behind a large brown desk. Terry had forgotten he was even there. "I didn't mean for you to stop at the door. Come over here."

Terry hurried closer, stopping a few feet in front of the desk.

"I'm Colonel Bishop. You must be Terrance," said the man. "I've been wondering when you were going to show up." He wore a pair of thin glasses and had one of the larger pads in his hand. "Already seven. Imagine that."

"Yes, sir," Terry said, remembering the doorman's words.

The colonel was a stout man, a little wider than the others. He was older too, Terry guessed. He may have been tall, but it was difficult to tell without seeing his whole body. "I expect you're hoping to begin your classes now," said Bishop.

"Yes, sir," he said.

"You say that, but you don't really know what you're saying yes to, do you?"

The question seemed more like a statement, so Terry didn't answer. He only stood there. Who was this man? Was this how school was supposed to be?

"Terrance, let me ask you something," said the colonel, taking a moment. "Did your mother tell you anything about this program you're going into?"

Terry thought about the question for a moment. "Um, she said you come to school on your birthday," he said. "And that it's just like it is at home, except there's more kids like me."

Colonel Bishop blinked. "That's right, I suppose. What else did she say?"

"That when it was over, I get to go back home," he said.

"And when did she say that was?"

Terry didn't answer.

Colonel Bishop cocked an eyebrow. "Well? Didn't she say?"

"No, sir," muttered Terry.

The man behind the desk started chuckling. "So you don't know how long you're here for?"

"No, sir."

Colonel Bishop set the pad in his hand down. "Son, you're here for the next ten years."

A sudden rush swelled up in Terry's chest and face. What was Bishop talking about? Of course Terry was going home.

He couldn't stay here. "But I promised my sister I'd be home today," he said. "I have to go back."

"Too bad," said the colonel. "Your mother really did you a disservice by not telling you. But don't worry. We just have to get you started." He tapped the pad on his desk, and the door opened. A cluster of footsteps filled the hall before two large men appeared, each wearing the same brown coats as the rest. "Well, that was fast," he said.

One of the men saluted. "Yes, sir. No crying with the last one. Took her right to her room without incident."

Terry wanted to ask who *the last one* was, and why it should be a good thing that she didn't cry. Did other kids cry when they came to this school? What kind of place *was* this?

"Well, hopefully, Terrence here will do the same," said Bishop. He looked at Terry. "Right? You're not going to give us any trouble, are you?"

Terry didn't know what to do or what to say. All he could think about was getting far away from here. He didn't want to go with the men. He didn't want to behave. All he wanted to do was go home.

But he couldn't, not anymore. He was here in this place with nowhere to go. No way out. He wanted to scream, to yell at the man behind the desk and his two friends, and tell them about how stupid it was for them to do what they were doing.

He opened his mouth to explain, to scream as loud as he could that he wouldn't go. But in that moment, the memory of the doorman came back to him, and instead of yelling, he repeated the words he'd been told before. "No, sir," he said softly.

Bishop smiled, nodding at the two men in the doorway. "Exactly what I like to hear."

Get the Amber Project now, exclusively on Amazon

GET A FREE BOOK

Chaney posts updates, official art, previews, and other awesome stuff on his website. You can also follow him on Instagram, Facebook, and Twitter.

Search for **JN Chaney's Renegade Readers** on Facebook to join the group where readers can come together and share their lives and interests, especially regarding Chaney's books.

For updates about new releases, as well as exclusive promotions, sign up for the VIP mailing list. Head there now to receive a free copy of *The Other Side of Nowhere*.

https://www.subscribepage.com/organic

Enjoying the series? Help others discover *The Constable* series by leaving a review on Amazon.

BOOKS BY J.N. CHANEY

Renegade Star Series:

Renegade Star

Renegade Atlas

Renegade Moon

Renegade Lost

Renegade Fleet

Renegade Earth

Renegade Dawn

Renegade Children

Renegade Union

Renegade Empire (April 2019)

Renegade Prequels:

Nameless

The Constable

The Constable Returns (April 2019)

The Last Reaper Series:

The Last Reaper

Fear the Reaper (March 2019)

The Orion Colony Series:

Orion Colony

Orion Uncharted

Orion Awakened

Orion Protected (April 2019)

The Variant Saga:

The Amber Project

Transient Echoes

Hope Everlasting

The Vernal Memory

Standalone Books:

Their Solitary Way

The Other Side of Nowhere

ABOUT THE AUTHOR

J. N. Chaney has a Master's of Fine Arts in creative writing and fancies himself quite the Super Mario Bros. fan. When he isn't writing or gaming, you can find him online at **www.jn-chaney.com**.

He migrates often but was last seen in Avon Park, Florida. Any sightings should be reported, as they are rare.

The Constable is his eighteenth novel.

53429853R10171

Made in the USA
Columbia, SC
15 March 2019